BETTER

the

DEVIL

YOU KNOW

MAYA DANIELS

BOOKS

By Maya Daniels

The Broken Halos Series

The Devil is in the Details

Speak of the Devil

Encounter with the Devil

The Devil in Disguise

To Look the Devil in the Eye

Better the Devil You Know

Give a Devil His Due

Vinci Books

vinci-books.com

Published by Vinci Books Ltd in 2025

1

A CIP catalogue record for this book is available from the British Library.

Paperback ISBN: 9781036706708

The EU GPSR authorised representative is Logos Europe, 9 rue Nicolas Poussion, 17000 La Rochelle, France contact@logoseurope.eu

Chapter One

RAPHAEL

"I failed you, Zedkiel."

My arms tremble where I'm pressing my balled knuckles on the cold stone, while my head is bowed in the destroyed building of what we have called Sanctuary for centuries. Blood trickles from my wounds, thick fat drops splattering before my eyes. Cold seeps into my legs where I kneel, my chest hollow like a gaping hole. Shivers rake my spine and shoulders, claws shredding my insides with despair.

"I failed to stop you from your madness when you sacrificed everything to bring her to life, and I failed you now when I didn't protect her."

Rasping the words, I dig my nails in the skin of my palms, hoping that will make me feel other pain than the one in my soul. The emptiness inside me grows like a hungry beast insatiable for my suffering, ready to swallow me whole.

I lost my charge.

I lost Zedkiel's daughter.

A shuddering breath fills my shriveling lungs.

"What have we done, Zedkiel?" The silence is so oppressive, my shoulders bow deeper from the weight of it. "What have we done?" I whisper to the cracked, splintering ground.

"It's little too late to be wondering what you've done now, Raphael."

"Did you come here to gloat?" I don't need to turn to see Beelzebub, so I stay as I am, my forehead pressed on the unforgiving ground. "Go ahead, tell me how I failed Helena."

"Not even I am that cruel, *brother*."

"Is this how you felt?" The sincerity in his words makes me tilt my head so I can see him, albeit upside down, from where I'm kneeling. "When you were sent to Hell. Is this how you felt? Like you were not good enough to stay so you were sent away? Did you all feel this emptiness spreading inside you destroying your will to live?"

"Is that what you think?" Leaning his meaty shoulder on the part of a wall that's still standing, he folds his arms over his chest, his red eyes narrowed at my face. "Is that what all of you have been thinking since the beginning of time? That we were not good enough to stand by your side?"

"I failed her, Beelzebub. I failed them both …" Ignoring his comment, my eyes close in agony. It doesn't matter how they feel, how any of us feel about anything.

"Let me know when you are done feeling sorry for yourself so we can get moving," he spits in disgust. "Just make it fast. The wards might be broken but standing here makes my stomach churn."

"It's the sacred ground it was built on." I don't know why I feel the need to tell him what he already knows.

"It's seeing you looking pathetic like that, not the damn ground." A humorless laugh booms out of his chest. "The

Great Raphael, a slobbering fool kneeling in the middle of ruins. Oh, how the mighty have fallen."

"How dare you! She cared about you … she cared enough, she fought to save your life." Lifting up on my knees, I push the words through clenched teeth. "You dare laugh at my pain for losing her?"

"See"—Jabbing a finger at me, he glares, his red eyes flashing with anger—"that's your problem right there. You think you are the only one that lost Helena. That's always been your problem, the lot of you up there on your high horses in Heaven. Selfish bunch of fuckers."

"I know you cared about her."

"Of course, I fucking cared you stupid fuck." His form blurs when he spins around, his fist connecting with the wall and sending bricks and rubble exploding all around him. My arms lift to protect my head. "She saw something in me that none of you cared enough to see. Something worthy enough that she risked her life and everything she believed in so she could protect my life. Me … one of the rulers of Hell."

"I failed you, too." My head hangs in shame.

"You need to snap out of it or I'm going to pummel you to death myself." Beelzebub's words are flat enough to jerk my head up, so I look at him. "Do you know what is happening out there?" His arm shoots out, pointing in a random direction. "Do you know what has befallen your beloved humans after she was gone?"

"My brothers will deal with whatever it is. I'm no good for anyone." I clench my jaw, my nostrils flaring as I hold back the unshed tears burning my eyes.

"Your pain is not worse than what Shadow is dealing with. He had to kill his mate to honor her wishes." Beelzebub takes a step in my direction, his body coiled with tension. "Nor is it worse than what Satanael is suffering right now. He watched his daughter breathe her last breath in front of his eyes. I can't control them both, and I need help. So, you better do what you need to do to pull yourself together and fast. Or all of us are doomed."

"You should let them grieve Beelzebub." A sharp pain stabs my chest and doubles me over. I blink away tears. "Let them grieve for the one that protected everyone, the one none of us could protect."

"Do you know where Satanael is?" I lift my head to look at him when he asks the question casually, contradicting his anger and aggressive posture. "Well? Do you?" His chin tilts up, prompting me to answer.

I frown at his unusual behavior. "No."

"Oh, splendid." Bending slightly at his waist, he glares at me. "He went back to Hell! Do you know why, Raphael? No?" He gets louder and louder with each word. "To find her in Hell. He thinks his daughter is in the pits of Hell, and he will turn it upside down to find her!"

"She is not in Hell." Anger surges through me, and my fist connects with the ground, shuddering whatever is left of the building while cracking and splintering the ground.

"You think he doesn't know that? He tried Heaven first, and when he couldn't go through the portal, he found the next best thing, leaving nothing but blood and bodies behind." Sucking in a gulp of air, his face reddens. "Do you know where Lucifer's sons are, Raphael?" undeterred by my anger, Beelzebub takes another step, his glower deepening. "I'm glad you asked. They are roaming the human realm and killing everything that crosses their path, blaming the humans and rogues for what happened to her while looking for djinn."

"No …" A numbness overtakes my whole body, my skull

tingling from what I'm hearing. "Eric would never do something that would displease Helena, even after she was gone." My words are barely a breath passing my lips.

"Eric never would, *brother*. But that male out there is not the Eric we know. It's the Prince of Hell that just lost his mate. I can't get you to see reason, so do you think he will listen to me right now?"

"What have we done …"

"We all fucked up, that's what we did." His body shimmers and grows in front of my eyes before he takes control of himself. With fists clenched at his sides and lips pressed in a firm line, he takes a moment to collect himself before speaking again. "Get up and let's fix this. The end of days will fall upon us if we don't."

"Helena was the balance …" My words trail off as I search his face, and my stomach plummets to my feet. In my grief, I push away what losing her will mean for the realms.

"And now she's gone." Looking me square in the eye, Beelzebub nods. "It's chaos out there. If the human realm falls, we all go down. Heaven and Hell alike. Time will restart itself again … from the beginning."

Rubbing both hands harshly over my face, the feeling in my body slowly returns like a million ants crawling over my skin. It brings the pain back tenfold. Not a feeling I like, but the numbness is gone at least. My blood pounds through my veins, the sound deafening in my ears. The hammering of my heart against my ribs moves my body with its erratic beat.

"Helena said that the clocks in Lucifer's home started working when she was visiting Hell." Swallowing thickly, I look back at him. "She said they were ticking … Damn it all! I should've seen it before. She saw Death start the countdown on her life and I ignored it." My eyes dart left and right, my mind spinning.

"None of us thought anything of it." My gaze snaps to his. "We need to stop this."

"Yes." Collecting myself, I push off the ground, wavering when I stand up on my feet. "We need to fix it."

"Easy, Raphael." He is next to me in a flash, grabbing my arm to hold me up. "You are good to no one if you can't stand on your feet."

'I'm fine. I was kneeling too long." Ducking my head, I hide my gaze from his, pretending I'm brushing off the ruined pants I'm wearing. "Let's go find Eric."

"You are sure you can walk?" Turning my back on his question, I stride away so he doesn't notice something is not right.

What I'm planning to do will infuriate even him. What I'm planning to do will bring me lower than the pits of Hell. But I know now that it's the only way out of this. The only way to stop the worlds from collapsing and to save all our lives.

"Raphael?" The concern is like a dagger in my chest.

"I'm fine, Beelzebub. Just a lapse of judgment on my part. The realms and the human world are more important than my failure. Let's go find Shadow."

"I knew you'd see reason." Slapping my shoulder, Beelzebub sighs.

I hope this is seeing reason … I hope I don't doom us for all eternity. The thought is like a prayer in my mind as we leave the Sanctuary behind.

Chapter Two

HELENA

Stumbling around, I ignore the stinging pain on the soles of my bare feet where sharp pebbles and rocks are biting my skin. There is no strength left in me to lift my arms to keep my balance, leaving them hanging limply by my side. My head hangs low on my shoulders, the limp hair falling around my face and obscuring my vision.

Everything is gray.

Even the skin of my bruised and shredded skin where I watch my legs move one painfully slow step after another look devoid of any color. The cloth hanging like a sack over my bowed shoulders is gray as well. Moth-eaten holes spread over it like constellations of a million stars. Why do I feel so tired? Even taking a breath feels like a chore that I'm not sure I'd like to keep doing. Where am I? More importantly …

Who am I?

Someone bumps into my shoulder, sending me tattering forward. I barely manage to stay standing, hissing in pain when my bleeding feet slide through the sharp stones slicing my skin open. My head grazes someone's back, sending them stumbling ahead as well. With great effort, I lift my face up and look around. Sharp pain spreads from my neck through my shoulders, opening my mouth in a silent scream.

Blinking fast, I try to clear my blurry vision, my eyes burning from the effort where my dry eyelids rasp over them. Dozens of people move as slow and as lifeless as me. I'm surrounded by them from all sides, all of us moving at the same pace through what looks like a tunnel. In the dim light—just enough so it's not pitch black—I watch the heads move forward. What the hell is this place, and how did I get here?

In my confusion, I must've stopped because someone bumps into my back, propelling me forward. A whimper escapes me when my arms shoot out to stop me from falling. The moment my fingers tangle into the sack the person in front of me is wearing, a surge of energy zaps through me, setting my skin on fire. My anguished shriek bounces off the tunnel walls, splitting the silence like a blade.

All heads turn my way at the piercing sound. The air freezes in my lungs when dozens of gazes lock on mine, all of them wide-eyed and all of them on my own face, like a black and white photograph frozen in place. Like standing surrounded in a room full of mirrors, my face stares back at me everywhere I turn. My sluggish heart kicks up, battering my ribs hard as I shrink away from it and plaster my back on the damp wall of the tunnel.

Hands trembling, I dig my nails in the moldy stones of the wall, ignoring the pain when they break and rip off of my nailbeds. Fear like I've never felt before spreads through me, the tremors causing my body to shake so hard my knees almost buckle and send me tumbling on the ground. Numbness washes over me like a gust of wind.

My head whips around, each breath coming faster than the one before it and making me hyperventilate. Dizziness sweeps though me, my vision wavering and blurring everything in front of my eyes. All of them as one turn my way, taking a step closer. Something in me snaps, and I can feel it like a physical break of my sanity, the crack so loud it makes my ears ring, which silences the whooshing sound of the blood rushing through my veins at least.

"No..." The word is but a whisper passing my dry, split lips.

Pushing off the wall, I barrel through the bodies inching ever closer to me. Heart hammering behind my ribs, I yank and shove, heading in the direction of the only way forward. Hands reach out, fingers snagging at my neck and tangling in the strands of my limp hair while trying to hold me back. Panic makes me flail wildly, and I scratch at their faces, tearing skin and hair in my attempt to escape. Frantic from the fear, I don't pick a place where my claw-like fingers gauge any woundable place I can find. The dim light coming from in front of me like a beacon of hope is my only goal. I have to reach it to escape this madness.

More hands join the effort to hold me back. Hundreds of fingers menacingly grab at my arms, those that I've barreled through scraping their nails on the skin of my legs to keep me among them. Others wrap their hands around my long hair, yanking my head back and making my neck crack like a bullet in the deathly-silent tunnel. The harsh breaths passing my lips sound like a freight train mixing with the swooshing sound in my ears.

I fight harder.

Ignoring the pain that tries to hold me back, I bite and

hit, pushing and scratching my way through bodies adamant to keep me here. That pinprick of light looks so far away, but my will to escape and save myself gives me strength I shouldn't have. Like a wild animal, I move forward, slipping on the rocks covered in my own blood. I have to get away.

I have to get out of here.

Whoever these people are get stronger as well. They hold my limbs firmly, their bodies more animated the harder I fight. Desperation makes me choke on a scream that refuses to be voiced. The herculean strength from just a moment ago is starting to desert me. My flailing is turning sluggish while theirs gets more frenzied. Thick strands of my hair are ripped from my skull, the warmth spreading where blood spills down my neck.

"No ..." My voice sounds strange to my ears. Like it doesn't belong here.

Knees buckling, I drop on the ground, the skin of my palms shredding as my hands slide through the sharp rocks littering the floor. Crawling between hundreds of feet, I shoulder my way forward. It can't be that far, the pinprick of light in the distance. I just need to get there. I know it.

Abandoning their attempt to hold me back, the bodies around me start throwing themselves on my back. My forearms grind on the floor, spilling more of my blood when the weight slams my chest down. My chin shreds when it hits the ground hard, rattling my brain. Dark spots dance in front of my eyes, blood loss causing my head to swim and everything to spin in fast circles. In a last-ditch effort, determined to stay alive, I pull my hands under my chest. Pressing my palms as hard as I can over the unforgiving rocks, I shove myself up, my teeth cracking from the way I grind them. Holding my breath, my lungs burning, I bow my back while jerking up.

"Eric!"

The desperate scream is so loud that the tunnel shudders and trembles under me. A blast of something bursts from my chest, throwing everyone away, their bodies hitting the walls with resounding thuds. A crazed laugh echoes around me, curdling the blood in my veins. The ground under my hands and knees disappear and sends me tumbling through the air until my body hits something hard. Tiny grains of sand dig into my wounds and fill my mouth.

"Again," a deep, amused voice says, and I lift my head slightly, squinting at the harsh light to see who it is. I only see a blurry outline of a figure before my head drops down and everything goes black.

Blinking fast, I try to clear my vision.

Everything is devoid of color.

Stumbling around, I ignore the stinging pain on the soles of my bare feet where sharp pebbles and rocks are biting into my skin. There is no strength left in me to lift my arms to keep my balance, leaving them hanging limply by my side. My head hangs low on my shoulders, the limp hair falling around my face obscuring my vision.

Everything is gray.

Even the skin of my bruised and shredded skin where I watch my legs move one painfully slow step after another, look devoid of any color. The cloth hanging like a sack over my bowed shoulders is gray as well. Moth-eaten holes spread over it like constellations of a million stars. Why do I feel so tired? Even taking a breath feels like a chore that I'm not sure I'd like to keep doing. Where am I? More importantly …

Who am I?

Someone bumps into my shoulder, sending me tattering forward. I barely manage to stay standing, hissing in pain when my bleeding feet slide through the sharp stones and slice my skin open. My head grazes someone's back, sending them stumbling ahead as well. With great effort, I lift my face up, looking around. Sharp pain spreads from my neck through my shoulders, opening my mouth in a silent scream.

In all that pain, a thought pushes to the front of my mind. A name. My heart does a painful thump at the thought of that name. Something I should remember. I think I called that name out. Urgency makes me struggle to shake off the confusion.

Who am I?

What was the name I need to remember?

Chapter Three

RAPHAEL

Grinding my teeth, I glare at all the destruction around me. My feet slow down, my gaze sweeping the street for any indication that someone lurks in wait.

"No one is around here." Beelzebub takes the lead, striding ahead of me. "If you saw Shadow, you'd understand why."

"Then why are we here?" It takes effort to speak.

From the Sanctuary to the safe house, all I found was death. Charred buildings, destroyed neighborhoods, and dead bodies littering the streets. If I didn't know better, I would think the horsemen are running rampant in the human realm.

But that can't be.

If they are out of their slumber, all my brothers and sisters will be here fighting to stop them. Our very existence depends on it. Eric, on his own, even with Colt by his side, couldn't have done this in a matter of days. Dread eats at me as I follow Beelzebub, who still hasn't answered my question.

"Did you not hear what I asked?" hissing at him, I resist the urge to throw my fist at his head.

"I heard you." He keeps walking, not even looking my way. "You left your precious gifted children here. Or have you forgotten about them, too?" Stomping angrily, he clenches his fists and murmurs under his breath. "I wish I could forget about the damn pains in my ass."

"The hunters are still here?" Guilt stabs me hard, and it's followed by fury as I hurry after him. "Why are they not out protecting the humans?"

"How should I fucking know?" Glaring at me over his shoulder, Beelzebub clenches his jaw. "If they were doing what they are born to do, I wouldn't have come looking for you. It looks to me like those of us *unworthy* of your precious Heaven are the only ones doing their job right."

"What's that supposed to mean?" Grabbing his shoulder, I jerk him to a stop. "No one could've predicted that the djinn would do this."

"I'm not talking about the djinn." Getting in my face, he bumps his chest to mine aggressively. "I shouldn't be babysitting your experiments, *brother*. I'm a ruler of Hell, I should thrive on your incompetence. I should do what I was made to do. Yet here I am, playing a peacemaker with my tainted blood."

"How enlightening that I can manage to hurt your feelings." My mouth twists in displeasure at his childish behavior. "I have failed my role, too. Does that make you feel better?"

"You really are a stupid fuck." Taking a step back, he looks me up and down. "I have no desire to prove anything. As a matter of fact, I was quite happy with how things were, before that stupid girl decided it was a good idea to waltz through Hell like she owns the place. This is why I don't get tangled in anyone's politics." Throwing both hands in the air, he huffs. "All I want is for you to fix this shit. I just want to keep kicking, and I'm not looking forward to the wars we had at the beginning of time."

"It has nothing to do with Helena?" Tilting my head, I search his glowering gaze.

"It has everything to do with Helena!" he roars in my face so suddenly it forces me to take a step back. "That girl is a poison created to destroy us all. And she succeeded."

My lips twitch at the corners.

Beelzebub seethes.

My smile grows at his red face.

"She made me fucking care for her." Spitting the words, he rubs his hands roughly over his face. "I hate her because she made me care."

My mind is spinning with one thought after another while I watch the anguish swirl in his eyes. He tries to hide it, but I see it. It's right there in the depths of his soul, in the strain on his face, and in the slight bow of his shoulders. I'm still not sure he will agree with what I have in mind, no matter how destroyed he is from the loss of Helena.

With one last look, I turn away from him, heading for the safe house. "Come, let us see why the hunters are hiding behind wards."

After a second of hesitation, he falls in step with me. Pain and anger waft off him like from a furnace and feeds my own. How could everything have gone so wrong? The girl was important, yes. But no one knows how integral she is to all of us, like a linchpin holding it all together.

Now everything is falling apart like dominoes pushed over by the slightest breeze.

Urgency tingles my spine and the back of my head. My shoulders are itching to release my wings and go swinging at everything and everyone, as well. I must play this right if I'm to succeed in doing the impossible. Ignoring the clenching of my heart at the thought and the consequences my actions are about to bring, I steel my resolve. *It's the only way,* I tell myself as I near the safe house. If I say it enough times, I might just make it real.

Pushing the front door open, my feet falter for a second. An oppressive feeling washes over me like impending doom. Shaking the feeling off, I square my shoulders and march through the house with a purpose. It won't do any good if they see me crumbling under my own loss and pain.

Hushed voices lead me to the common room where everyone gathers. Beelzebub is like a silent shadow at my back, doing his best to keep what he is feeling in check. I should follow his example. All chatter stops when we step into the room. Twenty or so faces tilt up, staring at us with emotions ranging from shock to hatred. Well, that's a new one for me. I've never been loathed by humans. It's eye-opening and punctuates Beelzebub's words from earlier.

"Raphael." George straightens from where he is leaning on the wall with his arms folded over his chest. "I thought you were dead."

The hunter has the decency to look ashamed at my raised eyebrow. Standing just a step inside the room, I glance at all of them in turn, anger rising with each face I see. When my gaze lands on the girl, Helena's friend, she lifts off the floor slowly. Cass, I believe her name is. She is the only one watching me with hope in her large brown eyes while her dark curls bounce around her head with her movement.

"I knew you'd come for us." She gives me a hesitant smile that does not reach her eyes. "Tell us what to do."

"There is nothing we can do, you stupid bitch." Another

man snarls from the side, jumping to his feet. "He needs to fix this shit they created with that abomination we should've killed from day one."

"See what I mean?" Beelzebub pipes in casually from behind me.

"And what abomination is that, human?" Punctuating the word "human" snaps his head in my direction, a frown bunching his forehead.

I remember this hunter. This is the one that was giving Helena a hard time when she was only trying to keep them safe. My eyes narrow at him, seeing him squirm under my scrutiny.

"Hel. A fitting nickname, don't you think, Raphael?" Sneering at me, he balls his fists at his sides.

"Do not say my name as if we are old friends, hunter." My softly spoken words widen his eyes, his bravado faltering. "You have forgotten your place, I see."

"I can help him remember, *brother*." Beelzebub cracks his neck, the laughter evident in his voice.

Keeping my eyes locked on the hunter, I lift my hand up to halt Beelzebub. Something akin to triumph glints in the human's gaze, as if I have just proven him right about something. Great sadness settles in me with that. How have we left things to get this lousy right in front of our noses? Has the faith in us dwindled so much that humans are sneering at us now? Shoving the thought away to the back of my mind where it belongs, I clench my jaw.

My wings burst from my shoulder blades, spreading around me like an ominous cloud. Feathers rustling, I shake them open, stretching them as wide as they will go. My glow intensifies, illuminating the dimly lit space. The awe on their faces sickens me. Especially on the face of the one daring to use my name like it's his God-given right.

George and Cass are the first ones to drop on one knee and bow their heads. My power blasts from me, making the rest of them shudder before they do the same. I feel Beelzebub shiver behind me even though he's hidden by my wings, but he wisely says nothing of my display.

"You dare hide here while humanity needs you?" My voice is no longer my own, the power given to me by Heaven echoing like a million voices speaking as one. "You dare turn your back on what you were born to do?"

"I will not let demons feast on my soul." To my shock, the sneering hunter is capable of speaking under the onslaught of my power. "I would rather die here than step a single foot out there." His whole body is shaking with his effort to hold his head up.

My head tilts at his words. "You think your soul belongs to you to do as you wish?" My heart breaks at the hatred in his gaze. My own will be cast down from Heaven for what I'm about to do. "You believe it was given to you so you can choose what to do with it? You breathe to protect humanity and nothing more."

"No!" Spittle flies from his sneering lips.

"Very well." looking down at him, keeping my face blank, I flick my hand, stabbing pain spreading through my chest.

The hunter's eyes widen in fear before they lose the spark, and he drops lifeless on the floor. The silence is like daggers repeatedly piercing my skin. Beelzebub sucks in a shocked breath, which only makes the whole situation worse.

"Anyone else willing to die now instead of fighting?" Not one head lifts to answer me. "I suggest you all start moving." Pulling back my power, I watch them sag before scrambling to their feet.

"We will not let you down." George squares his shoulders, jerking his head at the rest of them. They stand frozen as they stare at me blocking the door.

"You know what you have to do?" Seeing that he took the leadership of them, I squint at him.

"Yes, Archangel." Clenching and unclenching his fists, he meets my eyes. "We will start at the first sighting of demons."

With a sharp nod, I fold my wings in and step out of the way. Opposite me, Beelzebub does the same, but I avoid his searching gaze. The hunters bolt out of the room like it's on fire, belting their weapons as they leave. George gives a firm nod as he walks past, making the girl the only one left in the room with us.

Cass stands still, looking at me again with that hope bright in her gaze. Standing still, I ignore it, although every second is like an eternity pressing on my shoulders. When she reluctantly comes closer to me, my whole body stiffens. Her head lifts slowly, fingers twitching as she reaches for my forearm. I barely manage to not jolt from her touch.

"Please, bring her back." Swallowing thickly, her fingers tighten on my arm. My eyes snap to hers, watching a tear trickle from the corner of one eye. "I'm begging you … bring her back."

My throat tightens when she drops her hand and runs out of the room. Heart thundering in my chest, I finally look at Beelzebub. He stands still, his unblinking eyes on my face. After what feels like forever, he gives me a sharp nod and leaves me standing alone.

Time just started ticking in my race against fate.

I pray I get to the end before the last domino drops.

Chapter Four

ERIC

Dropping the dead rogue demon at my feet, my head swivels to the side where Colt snarls, pulling another one limb from limb. Their shrieks are feeding my rage, fanning the inferno burning in my chest. I can feel the blood streaming down my face and heaving chest, tickling my skin. Pivoting on my foot, I search the area for more.

More rogues, more humans … it matters not how, or what they look like. The djinn that took the only thing I cared about are among them. All of them will die, so I don't miss the fuckers. I will bathe the realms in blood.

"No more." Colt's voice is distorted from the long fangs filling his mouth. His chest is rising and falling fast as he curls his upper lip in a snarl. "There is no one else here."

With a nod, I unfurl my wings and take to the air. It's easier to spot them from up here. Like vermin scrambling around hiding from the inevitable. Darkness spreads in me with each breath I take. I will take them all with me before I follow Helena. Just thinking her name makes me sway in the air, pitching sideways. Righting myself at the last moment, I feel the ground graze my wings. Wings I wouldn't have if it wasn't for her.

Whatever is left of my heart rips at that thought.

Death. That's all I want to see.

I want all of them dead for taking her from me.

My head jerks erratically in hopes to stop thinking. I don't want to think. I want to kill. Seeing Colt in the air brings my attention to what we are doing. I follow behind him, my eyes trained on the ground searching for any place someone can hide.

The sun is setting behind the ruined city. Broken buildings stick out from the ground like gnarled fingers trying to reach the orange orb to bring it down, or like hungry beasts so desperate for light they want to hold it with them forever. They are desperate because the shadows are coming. Baring my teeth at the broken towers, I curl my claws in glee. Shadows are what I rule. It's what will feed on all of them in just a moment. The terror that hangs heavy in the air nourishes me like a drop of water will sustain a thirsty plant.

The air stirs, a fresh scent filling my nostrils. What used to be my heart lurches painfully at it and I flip around expecting to be attacked. When nothing but empty sky greets me, a frown pulls the skin of my forehead over my eyes. I can still smell it, the too-pure power singeing my skin. I spin around fast again, circling the air with the same result. There is nothing here, just me hovering above the ruins with Colt long gone in search of more targets for our rage.

"Eric!"

Helena's voice screams inside my head so loud I plummet to the ground, my body cracking the already-destroyed pavement when I hit it. My hands cover my ears, expecting them to bleed from the horrified sound.

"Helena!" roaring her name, I shoot to the sky, rotating frantically while searching for her. "Helena!" Empty skies meet my gaze, but the scent hangs heavy in the air. I suck it in greedily as if that will bring her back into my arms.

And then it's gone.

The stench of death and decay makes me gag. My eyes water from it while I hold my breath, hoping to feel something, anything from her. When my head starts to swim because it's deprived of oxygen, I release it with a whoosh before screaming in rage. The silence around me gets thicker when the echoes of my scream fade away. My whole body is trembling, suspended midair.

A heavy weight settles like a rock over my chest, and I lower myself down until my feet touch the ground. Tremors rake my spine, everything blurring in my vision. Clenching my clawed hands, I relish the pain when my sharp talons dig deep into my skin, ripping it to shreds.

"I must say I'm very disappointed." I whirl around, snarling at the one speaking. "I'm assuming I should be afraid for my life?"

Throwing myself at him, ignoring the alarms blaring in my skull that I should stop and think, my fists are a blur. Bone crunches under my onslaught, yet I keep punching with every ounce of fury burning my soul. Someone slams into my side, flinging me off Raphael and breaking one of my wings in the process. The bones crunch, twisting in odd angels. Another roar shudders the ground when I jump to my feet, ready to kill both Archangels. Until I lock eyes with Beelzebub.

"He is not even fighting back, you fool!" Beelzebub spits in my face while stabbing a finger at Raphael, who is sprawled on the ground in a bloody mess. "Even you should have more honor than that."

"Honor?" Baring my teeth, I hold myself back with everything in me so I don't rip his head off. "You want honor from me after everything?"

"He didn't kill Helena." The calmness in Beelzebub's voice hurts more than if he ripped my wings from my back barehanded.

"No, I did!" snarling at him, I glare at both of them. "Because she wanted you safe."

"Nobody is safe right now, Shadow." Raphael's pained comment makes me roar with humorless laughter.

"Truth." Cocking my head, I grin at him. "I'm going to kill everyone eventually. None of you will live past the end of the week."

"How very thoughtful of you," Beelzebub drawls, his face twisted in disgust. Raphael lifts himself off the ground with a roll of his shoulders, wincing in pain.

"Get out of my way." The air whistles through my gnashed teeth when they both face me.

Raphael scowls at me and opens his mouth, but thankfully no words come out of it. The ground rocks and sways under my feet, the large cracks in the pavement splitting wider from the shudder. The Archangel and Beelzebub spread their arms to their sides, balancing on the balls of their feet. I know what this is, and at that realization, my mouth presses firmly in a thin line making my jaw hurt. No matter where I go, it eventually finds me.

"I told you to leave me alone," I snap, anger evident in my voice and the fact that I don't turn to face them.

"Me going away is not for you to decide, Shadow." What used to be a hissing voice now rumbles deep and robust like rocks rolling off a mountain. "I made a promise. I will see it through."

"Narsi?" Beelzebub's eyes are bulging out of his skull comically as he cranes his neck to look at the damn Haltija. I glance over my shoulder, watching the now monstrous-sized spirit nod jerkily.

"Beelzebub. You may bring some sense into his muddled brain." A grin spreads on the Haltija's face, his yellowed teeth beaming.

In hopes of protecting Helena, the Haltija grew in size and stayed that way. I couldn't care less what happens to him, but after she asked him to protect me, he has been at my heels no matter where I go. He scares the humans and demons alike before I get a chance to rip them apart, pissing me off to no end.

"Eric, I need you to think." Raphael, ignoring everything but what interests him as usual, takes a step closer to me. His split lip and eyebrow are healing as I watch, only smeared blood left on his skin.

"Eric no longer exists. Go back to your realm angel. Go stew in your own importance and holiness." Cracking my neck, I turn away from them, my feet putting space between us fast. "I have no time for any of you."

Terrified screams split the air from some distance away, and a grin grows on my face. Colt must've found strugglers, and the sound of their fear builds anticipation in me. A fist slams on the ground in front of me, cutting off my way. Jerking back a step, I spin, claws slashing at the exposed forearm taller than my body. My arm passes through it, the damn spirit turning incorporeal for a moment. I'm one of the larger demons in Hell, yet I look like a two-year-old standing next to an adult compared to the Haltija.

"Eric ..." Raphael calls out, but his words trail off when

Colt bursts from around the half-standing tower, dark wings flapping frantically in the air.

I swing up in the air to meet him, grinding my teeth when my still not healed wing pulls painfully on my back. Beelzebub and Raphael reach my brother faster, hovering in front of him like a living shield. I can feel the air stirring at my back when the Haltija ambles closer to us, as well.

"Three portals are opened two blocks down," Colt lisps through his bared fangs just as I push my way between the other two idiots standing in my way.

"Djinn?" The skin on my face pulls with my rage.

"No." Still panting, my brother locks his gaze on mine, and a shiver jolts up my spine from the horror in it. "All three are connected to each other. The pits of Hell are opened. Everything kept there for centuries is crawling out."

"I don't care what opened." I see Raphael and Beelzebub exchange a look from the corner of my eye. "It just means we need to kill faster. Let's not waste time."

"Have you completely lost your mind as well as your soul, Shadow?" Roaring, Raphael spins me around with a firm yank on my shoulder. Anger makes his angelic power sparkle and glitter around him threateningly.

I grin at him.

"At least you got my name right." Shaking off his grip, I half turn to my brother when his words freeze me.

"She will blame herself for what you are doing." Sadness drips like sap from his mouth, choking the air in my lungs as guilt claws my insides. "I hope you remember that … Shadow."

I don't breathe as I watch him turn away. My mind screeches to a halt with each flap of his wings, Beelzebub's and Colt's voices turning into a distant hum in my ears. I startle when a hand wraps around my middle, pulling me in front of the Haltija's scowling face.

"We need to follow the light one, Shadow." Putrid air washes over me from his breath. "He knows where my mistress is, but I cannot leave you behind. I have given my word."

Everything in me comes alert at those words, the high-pitched sound in my head deafening my ears. Coldness numbs my body, which sags in the spirit's hand. I search his determined face with unblinking eyes because I'm too afraid if my lids close for just a second what he said will be only a dream. The skin around his eyeless sockets pulls in mocking amusement.

"What did you say?" My lips barely move with the whispered question. I can feel my brother and Beelzebub at my back, the Haltija getting their attention as well.

"The Archangel is going to find my mistress. I shall go with him, but I cannot leave you behind." My skin prickles from the evil grin lifting his mouth at the corners. "I can eat your face if you don't do what I ask. She is more important to me than you are, even if I fail to keep my oath to her."

Beelzebub's barked out laugh jerks my head away from the Haltija. My lips pull in a sneer that only makes him double over in the air. He is lucky the spirit tightens his fingers around me, or I would've ripped off his wings.

"I should've found Narsi first." Beelzebub gasps for air, thumping his chest. "He puts things into a great perspective really fast." The damn Haltija grins happily at the phrase.

"What is going on here?" Colt looks as confused as I feel.

"If the pits of Hell have opened, it means Satanael has already reached them in his search for Helena." All humor evaporates from Beelzebub's face.

"He was searching?" My body is twitching, but whether from shock or surprise I can't decide.

"While you decided to go on a killing spree and while Raphael was drowning in his own guilt, Satanael went searching for her. I tried to tell you, but you know how well that went."

Urgency overtakes every thought process as I look at the Haltija. "Find Raphael!"

Chapter Five

HELENA

Blinking rapidly, I stare at my dirty, blood-crusted, shuffling feet in confusion. Something important tries to penetrate the cotton filling my head, making my temples throb with a splitting headache. The dim light stabs my dry eyes, forcing me to blink faster, my eyelids rasping like sandpaper over them.

I feel so tired.

Unable to hold my head up, it rolls on my shoulders, hanging heavily to my chest. Something inside me pokes insistently, raising panic like I know something is about to happen but I can't remember what.

Why can't I remember?

Tilting my face to the side, I fight the drowsiness the best I can so I can look around me. Grinding my teeth when sharp rocks slice the skin of my bare feet, I startle when I notice the person next to me. With great difficulty, I lift my head up to see the dozen or more bowed heads moving forward in a tunnel. Everything is gray, including the papered-with-holes limp sacks all of us are wearing. I can't remember my own name, but a thought jolts me like a hundred watts stiffening my spine. *I wouldn't be seen dead dressed like this.*

I snort.

The sound makes everyone stop, and I bump into the person in front of me. Stumbling back, my foot steps on the person behind me, pinballing me from one body to another. My eyes dart around expecting them to be angry with me for my clumsiness.

None of them move, the hair so much like mine hanging like a curtain around them and hiding their faces. Uneasiness drops my stomach to the floor. Something is about to happen. A déjà vu feeling prickles the back of my skull, and I slink away until my back hits the jutting damp rocks of the tunnel wall. Cold sweat dribbles down my spine, beading on my hairline and upper lip. Wiping my sweaty palms off the sack covering my body, I fist the fabric between my fingers. Raspy grinds scrape the skin of my palms, and I jerk my head down, lifting my hands to my face.

A few grains of sand stand out starkly in the dim light and grayness around me. Frowning, I pick them off and roll them between my fingers. The cotton in my head clears slightly, bringing with it a bright light. A weightless feeling like I'm falling through space spreads through me while a peal of menacing laughter raises goosebumps over my arms and legs and … and … a name.

"Arghhh …" My frustrated growl for being unable to remember snaps all the heads in my direction.

Fear sends a jolt through me when everywhere I turn my face is staring back at me like dozens of mirrors facing me no matter where I go. Fisting my hands to stop them from trembling presses the sand in my skin, embedding it in my fingers. Something stirs in my chest like bubbling lava. Thick and dangerous, it swirls ominously, lodging my heart in my throat.

The ground trembles under my feet, pitching everyone around me to stumble unsteadily. Pictures flash behind my eyes of a handsome face looking down at me with green eyes sparkling in humor. My heart lurches, punching my ribs painfully. My lips tingle with the thought of a name. The feeling of loss almost cripples me when those green eyes hover at the front of my mind. Lips parting to say his name, I'm stopped when hands surge for me, grabbing my limbs and dragging me down.

Everything in me screams that I need to fight them. I need to get away. Yet, I allow them to push me on the dusty, rock-laden ground without a protest. My face is shoved hard, the skin of my cheek ripping on a sharp shard of a rock and wetting the floor with my blood. I stay limp, eyes unblinking with that green gaze looking back at me. The hands and broken nails yank on my hair and tear at my exposed skin, but I'm so detached I don't feel any pain.

Then something changes.

The green eyes I hold in the front of my mind like a life-line lose their sparkle. The humor and love that wards off the cold and pain and buries my despair, turn it into anguish. The pain I'm supposed to feel reflects in them and stabs me in the chest Trying to shift my head to see if my heart has been ripped out proves futile because I can't move. My rage-filled scream at the hurt in that gaze pierces the silence, and the ground under me disappears, hurling me through space.

My body bounces once with a grunt when I hit hard-packed sand. Blinding light burns my retinas, forcing my eyes closed as my mouth fills with sand. That evil chuckle clears my head, and all my focus turns on the sound. With great effort, I lift my head and blink through the brightness in hopes of finding out who it is. A figure looms nearby, but it's only an outline that I can see.

"Again." He sneers, sending ghostly fingers racing up my spine.

"This is a mistake," another voice I can't remember hearing before answers him. "She's fighting it. She remembers things."

"Impossible," the first one snaps. "She can't remember. I said again!"

Darkness covers me like a blanket, and I see no more.

Sitting on my haunches, I lean my back on the damp wall of the tunnel. All the people around me stand facing forward, their heads hanging low on their shoulders. It took many times coming back to this place, each one bringing more memories until I think I figure it out. Whatever this place is, it's like a movie someone keeps rewinding and playing again, featuring yours truly as the main actress. If I didn't look like some wild person who has been discovered living in a jungle with no human contact since the day I was born, I may even be flattered. Snickering at the thought, I clamp a hand over my mouth when everyone turns around to face me.

That's another thing I learn. As long as I don't make a sound, they just stand there like statues, and I don't get hurled through space where that damn bright light sears my retinas. I'm starting to think I'll go blind from it eventually. *Not if I keep my mouth shut and just chill here.* Snickering silently at my thought, I eye everyone warily. It does creep me out to see own face staring back with vacant eyes.

Not anymore.

Even if it's a nightmare, after the same one enough times there is a comfort in the familiarity of it, of knowing what to expect. Plus, I find the fact that I'll eventually open my eyes and do it all over again has its own perks. Another snicker passes my lips and hands reach for me.

My fingers curl around a sharp rock near my feet, and I hurl it at the closest face, the ribbed edge slicing the forehead open. "Keep your hands to yourself," I whisper, sneering nastily at the person.

The hands stop a breath away from grabbing me. I crouch, frozen, afraid any movement will spring them into action. When they keep standing like the chuckling asshole has pressed pause, a smile splits my face. This shit can be fun. I wonder if I whisper enough times will I be able to have them frozen in awkward positions? Cocking my head to the side, I debate the wisdom of that idea. Placing more weight on the back of my thighs, my butt nudges my foot forward, kicking a few rocks off the ground. The clinking sound sends a jolt through me a second too late.

Hands grab me, pushing me down while broken nails scrape and tear at my skin. My face is pressed hard on the sharp rocks, splitting the skin on my cheekbone open and wetting the ground with my blood. Bodies pile on top of me, and I know if I stay quiet, they'll crush me until I can't breathe. With my eyes staring unblinking, my high-pitched, shrill laugh fills the air.

The asshole said it's impossible for me to remember. My

laughter goes up in volume. I may not remember who I am and my own name, but I learn one thing about myself: never tell me I can't do something because I'll sure as hell prove you wrong.

The ground under me disappears, hurling me through space while my crazy laughter fills the air.

Chapter Six

RAPHAEL

Guilt suppressed by anger, I pump my wings furiously through the city. I shouldn't ignore all the portals opened from Hell that gape at me from the ground. Yet, I keep moving, my head swiveling on my shoulders while I search. Colt said the three connected portals from the pits of Hell were two blocks away. I left that behind me half a city ago yet, there are no signs of the hunters or an entrance to Heaven. Fear is trying to eat my insides like acid, churning in my stomach. Hope is pushing up to replace it, but I fight against it.

Hope is the Devil's trick.

What humans don't know is it's the biggest vice of them all. It feeds insanity to a level no fanatic can fathom. Hope will push them to a point where they sell their souls, convincing them it's the only way, all because they hope to get what they want or desperately need. A nice little trick on Satanael's part but not one I need. Not right now. Pandora should've kept what was left in her possession better protected.

Shadows too dense to be anything but solid forms move under the destroyed buildings. Veering to the side, I take a left and lower to the ground for a better look. A dozen or so figures dressed all in black move in synchronized formation, and that confirms my suspicions. These are the hunters I've been searching for. Ahead of them is a makeshift wall of broken vehicles and slabs of ripped-apart walls. Metal pipes and wires jutting out of it like spikes of barbed wire protect the humans huddled behind it. Between the humans and the hunters, monsters crawl the streets searching for their next victim.

Not just any monsters, no. My spine stiffens when I see creatures long forgotten roaming the human realm. They never should've been set free in Hell, little less among human flesh. Uncertainty wreaks havoc in my mind. I should stand with the hunters and protect humanity because that is what I was created to do. Helena's smile comes as clear as daylight in my head, and it's so much like her mother's that I grind my teeth together, hovering between the humans and hunters while unseen to their mortal eyes.

"Where are we going?" I whirl around, bracing for an attack at Eric's voice. He tilts his head in question, the double horns on the sides of his face glinting in the last dying rays of the sun. Behind him, Narsi looms, blotting out my view of the broken city.

"You came." I don't know why I'm surprised, but I am. I didn't think anything I said would get through his pain.

Fear flashes through his stony gaze, and he subtly clenches his fists to the sides. "The Haltija said you'll be looking for …" Swallowing thickly, a muscle jumps in his sharp jaw. "For Helena." His words end hoarsely.

My throat closes up at the anguish sharpening his features.

"She is not in Hell." My voice sounds harsh even to my own ears, and I wince.

Rearing like I've punched him, Eric glares at me. "Of course she isn't, you stupid fuck. You better have a way to bring me with you to Heaven. The Haltija said, you know where she is. You're not going anywhere without me." Spittle flies from his lips with his fury.

"She's not in Heaven, either ..."

Anything else I am about to say is cut off with the first shrill scream. We both snap our heads in the direction of the huddled humans. My breath chokes me when I see the nightmares crawling up the makeshift wall. They've reached the humans.

Eric stirs the air next to me, moving closer. I feel his eyes weighing heavily on my shoulders, pressing as hard as the guilt of failing everyone, including Heaven at this very moment. As I hover in the air watching the first human have his soul and flesh devoured by something none of us can name, my chest tightens, the beacon inside me that is connected to home stretching and tightening like a rubber band ready to snap at any moment. Despair closes my throat while the indescribable fear of losing everything clouds my mind.

Yet, I stand frozen as I watch the ground below dispassion-ately. My eyes are on the humans, the hunters still too far to come to their aid, but Eric is observing me. His searching gaze is like burning flames over my skin. I'm torn between fighting for humanity or following my hunch and searching for Helena. Will Beelzebub look at me with something akin to respect if he knows I'm not sure if I'm correct? Will Eric abandon his vengeance if he knows? As the feeling in my chest turns more painful, I can't help but selfishly wonder if I am willing to lose my place in Heaven on the off chance I'm right.

"You won't aid them." It's not a question, and the surprise in Eric's voice is a dagger in my heart.

"I need to find Helena." The sound of my voice does not betray my turbulent emotions.

Looking away from me, Eric surveys the ground before locking his gaze on the side of my face. Shame melts my insides, my wings rustling with it. I stare unseeing ahead of me at nothing.

"You know where she is." Again, not a question.

"Yes," I lie shamelessly, intensifying the pain in my chest.

"Let us aid the humans first then." His deep rumbling voice snaps my eyes to his face. He gives me a reproachful look, one side of his mouth, lifting in a rueful smirk. "You said it yourself. She will never forgive me for what I've done. I better start atoning for my sins, Archangel."

"You will do this before looking for her?" I have no idea why I'm even debating this, but I have the strong urge to ask.

"If I know one thing about my mate, Raphael, it's that she'll be fine for a bit longer no matter where she is." Angling his body towards the screaming voices below us, he shoots me one last look. "But if I don't do this, she will kick my ass all the way to Hell and back when she finds out. I'm not willing to risk it anymore."

My mouth gapes open as he shoots like a bullet from the sky and barrels right in the middle of the fight. Bright flashes of weapons being fired blink like stars in the dark-from-night city. Like an avenging angel, he sends creatures flying away from the makeshift wall as shadows jump to his aid. Monstrous roars join the human shrieks.

"Shall we join, Archangel?" Narsi's deep, gravelly voice accompanies his thudding footsteps that shudder the ground.

Taking a deep breath, I'm shocked to find the tightening in my chest eases a little. "Yes." Glancing at the Trowe, I smile hesitantly at his larger but still familiar scrunched up, wrinkled face. "Yes, we are joining him."

"Good." His eyeless sockets turn on my face, a grin showing off his yellowed teeth. "I'll eat their face." He chuckles happily.

A jolt of unease runs through me, and I blink a few times at his words. He is already ahead of me by the time I shake off the feeling. Another smile pulls on my lips. At least Helena won't say we didn't feed the Trowe in her absence. With a hard push of my wings, I join the fray.

Chapter Seven

HELENA

The rock I threw a second ago bounces off the forehead it is aimed at. "I told you to keep your hands to yourself," snapping angrily at the person wearing my face, I glare at her.

It takes quite a few times of me crouching like a scared little girl while trying my best not to make a sound until I have enough and say screw it. After that moment, I did everything from laughing to yelling, then I tried singing— that part held me here longest because I'm thinking they didn't want my off-key screeching near them—and dancing to test the boundaries. The more I rebel and fight the fog hiding my memories, the faster I go hurling through space and ending up here.

"Somebody is angry." Looking up at the roof of the tunnel, I snicker.

I don't know if the asshole that used to chuckle at me is watching me from up there, but I don't care. I feel unhinged. Not that I give a damn at this point since it doesn't look like I'm getting out of here anytime soon. But I'm so happy, my skin can barely contain me. Then, the idiot stopped chuckling. That asshole. Slapping the hand reaching for me away, I tilt my face at the roof again.

"You have anger issues, I think." Frowning, I rethink my comment. "No!" stabbing my finger at the roof, I grin widely. "You have inadequacy issues. That's it." High fiving myself, I shake my head, clumps of unbrushed hair flying all over the place. "I knew I'd figure you out."

No one answers me, all the people wearing my face crowding around me like some creepy dolls with their dull eyes and emotionless features. My fingers twitch, wanting to wrap around something, and I angle my head down so I can look at my thigh because I get an urge to reach there and take it. Take what, though? A weapon?

"Yes!" shouting triumphantly at the roof, I shake my fist at it. "I had a weapon and you took it, you coward." I have absolutely no idea if I'm telling the truth, but who cares? Let him come here to call me a liar so I can scratch his eyes out with my chipped and broken nails.

"Your accommodations also suck ass!" Slapping another hand away, I bend down, plopping heavily on the ground while wondering how much longer he will take this before he plunges me through space. I keep rumbling, anyway. "Don't get me wrong, I like all this"—Waving a hand carelessly, my eyes snag on the piece of broken nail hanging sideways and I start picking at it—"gray, absence of color crap you have going on. It's very …" Looking away from my destroyed nail, I squint at everyone around me as if they'll supply the word I can't think of. "Simplistic?" Tilting my head, I chew on the nail before gagging when I remember how disgusting my hands are. Spitting on the ground, I stick my tongue out, rubbing it on my forearm to clean the gunk. "Monochromatic?" The word is slurred because of my dry tongue when I continue my search for the term. It nags the shit out of me that I can't find the right one. "Anywho, as I was saying, it's cool and all, just boring." Giggling, I shiver slightly as I look around for where the draft can be coming from.

I see nothing but the idiots staring at me.

"But the inadequacy, that's not boring. It's quite intriguing, actually." Nodding to myself, I confirm the seriousness of my observation. "I've felt that way before. I might not remember why, but I know I have. The only difference is, I'm sure that I've had a better reason for it, or I would've stabbed your ass by now ..." trailing off, my eyes widen. "A sword, hmmm, no, that doesn't sound right." Staring hard at my fingers like they'll speak at any moment to help me out, I rack my brain, developing a headache all over again. "No! A dagger! That's it. That's what you took from me, you dumb shit."

Silence answers my revelation, but I don't care. I remembered one more thing. Progress is all that matters at this point. The headache gets worse, and something tickles my upper lip. Rubbing the back of my hand on it, I see red blood smeared on my skin. Blinking stupidly, it takes me a second to realize that it has color. It's not gray like everything else here. Grinning, I scrub my fingers under my nose in agitation.

"Hey, asshole! Why does my blood have color in your gray world?" Snickering, I keep my lips lifted despite the pain trying to split my head open. "That is the question." Lowering my voice dramatically, I add some humming for special effect. "To be, or not to be. That is the question."

My shrill laugh is cut off when I'm hurled through space.

This time I'm ready, so when my body collides with the hard-packed sand jarring my teeth, I roll over, biting my tongue in the process. Ending up on hands and knees, I hold my head low so I don't get blinded by the blaring light. My eyes still water from the sudden change, but I blink the stinging tears away. Through clumps of hair, I look at the chuckling asshole for the first time. My breath gets stuck in my lungs.

He can only be described as perfect.

Jet black hair is slicked back, coiled like a rope that falls over his shoulder down to his waist. High cheekbones accentuate his pointed chin and straight nose that sits above red, pouty, bow-shaped lips. Perfectly sculpted eyebrows and thick lashes make his violet eyes sparkle on his beautiful face. Muscly arms are crossed over his bare chest, while his bronze skin is stretched tight enough for me to see every muscle clearly. Silky pants cinched at his ankles hug strong thighs, ending with bare feet buried slightly in the sand. A glint in the bright light brings my eyes to his folded arms, where golden forearm protectors are wrapped all the way to his elbows.

I'd like to think, although I can't really remember anything apart from green eyes, that I've seen my fair share of handsome faces. But nothing like this guy. He is so perfect that my mouth keeps opening and closing soundlessly because I'm at a complete loss for words, which makes my brain dissolve into a useless puddle.

Seeing my stupefied state, his lips mimic a smile, and those violet eyes lock on mine. An emptiness so vast it pushes all the air out of my chest in a rush stares at me. There is nothing humane in this person. Not even a resemblance of emotion can be found on his perfectly molded face, apart from the mimicry he is performing for my sake. Just an empty void ready to devour everything in its path. This is not a twisted creature wanting to hurt everyone.

There is no reason behind whatever he is doing. It's evil for the sake of evil and nothing more.

A memory stabs the back of my eyes. I've seen perfection like this once. My perception flips, seeing a similar face while hanging suspended in the air looking at it upside down. A picture of a large stadium follows while I run through darkened hallways, my breath harsh in my ears.

The creature in front of me frowns just as I feel a trickle of blood dripping over my upper lip and wetting my mouth. Ignoring him, I focus on remembering more. I was searching for help because someone was hurt. Someone I can't think of not having at my side. Dark wings with a green glow at the tips of the feathers are enough to bring everything rushing back. My shaking hands give out, sending me face-first into the sand. With great effort, I push back up, rage burning so hot I think I might burst into flames.

"Djinn!" I spit at him like a curse, and he takes a startled step back. "How nice of you to show your face." A genuine grin splits my face.

"Impossible!" Glaring at me, his empty stare spreads cold through me.

A burst of light comes from the side, sparks flying everywhere and forcing both of us to shield our heads on reflex. When I pull my arm away, a swirling portal meets my eyes.

Chapter Eight

ERIC

My chest heaves with each harsh breath I take. Swiveling my head, I search for more creatures, but I see none. Further down to my right, Raphael is doing the same, his already shredded shirt now just a few straps hanging from his neck over his bloodied chest. Looking at him closer, I see one of his wings hanging lower on his back compared to the other. They must've tried to drag him down by pulling on it. My own blood trickles from the many wounds I suffered from vicious claws and talons.

"I think we are clear," Raphael calls out, and a human shrieks in answer from behind the debris they piled up in hopes of hiding. His face twists at the sound, and I can't help but laugh.

"Welcome to my world, angel. How does it feel to be feared?" Smirking at him, I survey the area again in case we missed one, spinning in place on my heel. "Narsi, I can't see shit from you on that side." The damn Haltija blocks more than half my view.

"It is clear, Shadow." His voice shakes the ground under

44

my feet, and he grins at me over his shoulder, black blood dripping down his chin. "I ate their face."

Scrubbing a hand over my face, I turn to Raphael when he ambles closer. "How Helena deals with him is beyond me."

"She has a gift to see the good if it's present and feed it like you'd feed flames." A sad smile lifts his mouth, but it's gone before it fully forms. "The hunters should be here by now." Squinting in the distance, he rubs the center of his chest. I frown at the movement.

"You doing okay? You're not severely injured, are you?" Giving him a once-over, I can't see a deep wound, only a few gashes on the side of his ribs.

"What?" The confusion clears from his face when he sees me watching him rub at his chest, and his arm drops to his side. "No, I'm not hurt." Clenching his jaw, he turns away and stalks down the street.

In two long strides I'm next to him, spinning him to face me with a harsh grip on his shoulder. "You are the only one that can lead me to her, Raphael. Don't be a stupid prick. If there is something wrong with you, I need to know."

"There is nothing wrong with me." Snarling, he yanks away from my hold. My eyebrows hit my hairline from the reaction. The natural golden glow around him is dimmed slightly but, that could be from exhaustion … I think.

"Is it the wing?" When he looks at me strangely, I point at the white feathers dragging on the pavement to his left.

"Oh." With a roll of his shoulders, the bones snap back in place as the appendage lifts, returning to its usual place. I stare at him. "That's nothing." He shrugs it off like it's an everyday thing and all of us can heal an almost ripped-off wing. "Short of ripping them off, my wings heal instantly."

"How convenient." At my drawl, he lifts an eyebrow.

"You sound bitter, Eric." Another almost smile pulls his mouth. "A perk of an Archangel."

"Right." I grind my teeth when the Haltija moves closer, shaking the ground. "Where to now?"

"First, we find the hunters to make sure they reach the humans. After that, we need holy ground." Answering me distractedly, his hand moves up towards his chest before he catches himself and lets it drop to his side.

"That's what you were looking for when I caught up with you? Holy ground?" The incredulity is unmistakable in my words.

"No. I have no idea what I was looking for." I just stare at him, and he huffs in frustration.

"Well?"

"What's with the interrogation Eric. The faster we find the hunters, the sooner we will be on our way." Growling obscenities, he takes to the air and I follow behind him.

Something is up with him, but he is right about one thing. We must find Helena first. Now that the fury and anguish from losing her have cleared, I want to ram my head in the nearest wall for not thinking of it sooner. When Helena's body disappeared from my arms, I didn't think anything of it. She is not human, so my brain connected that to her going to wherever beings like her will go. Actually, scratch that. I believed with everything in me that she left for Heaven where I'd never reach her. That was another thing fueling my desperation and my loss. Now that I know I can get to her, nothing else is important. Short of the Archangel keeling over, I'll let him keep his secrets. When we find my mate, she'll beat it out of him, anyways. I just know it.

Keeping Raphael in my sight, I follow behind searching for the hunters on the ground. Calling on my shadows, I spread them around like a cobweb looking to snag a fly. All humans have vices, secrets they hide even from themselves, but they can't hide them from me. It's easy to zone in on the ones we are searching for, especially with them protecting their darkness behind righteous disdain for my kind. Opening my mouth to call after Raphael, my nostrils fill up with that pure scent. It's so sudden that I drop through the air for a few feet before I catch myself. Flipping left and right, I search for the source but find nothing around. Just the dark sky and a blood-red full moon staring accusingly at me like it's my fault she is not bright and silver as she should be.

My head jerks when I shake it to clear my mind. I'm going to start thinking I'm insane if this keeps up. Sucking in air, I search for the scent, but it's gone like it never existed. *Yup, definitely going insane.*

With one last look around, I spot Raphael. "I found them." I push harder with my wings to reach him when he turns my way. "Just one block to the right. They have company."

The Archangel zooms in that direction without a word, and I'm right on his heels. If the sound coming from the earth below us is any indication, the Haltija is following. The humans might think a horde of angry elephants is upon them. We spot the hunters in the middle of a fight. Raphael plunges into it without a thought, his fists blurring when he squares off against the first demon. The ones fighting the hunters here are of Abaddon's ilk, high-class demons and much stronger than your typical rogue. The anger still turning my insides propels me faster, and I dive in with gusto.

Back to back with Raphael, we sync into coordinated movements or fists and kicks—or in my case, horns and claws. Sweat forms like a thin film over my skin, enough evidence that our opponents are no joking matter. There is no doubt in my mind that all the hunters would've died here tonight if we didn't reach them in time. A pained shout from a voice too familiar to my ears jerks my head in that direction, earning me bruised, if not cracked, ribs when the demon I'm fighting scores a solid kick. My hand shoots out, snagging him around the neck, cutting his victory grin short. My claws rip through his neck, the tendons of my forearm straining from the tough skin I pull apart. Dropping his lifeless body at my feet, I spin around looking for Cass. It was her that screamed in pain.

Sprawled on the ground, she stares in horror at the horned demon looming over her. His arm is lifted in the air, fingers curled with talons as long as my fingers ready for the killing blow. My shadows surge from my body, restraining his movement, and I sprint at him. He doesn't get a chance to see who snuffs his life before my hand sinks in his chest, ripping his heart out with a loud, squelching sound. Helena's friend is showered in blood as the demon topples to the side. The whites in her eyes stand out, stark on her blood-soaked face when she looks at me in shock.

"You need to stand up." Offering a hand, I wait palm up until she hesitantly wraps her shaking fingers in mine, being mindful of my claws. Shit, I probably look scarier to her than the one that tried to kill her. This is fucking Raphael's job, not mine.

"Eric?" Her hesitant whisper tightens my chest.

"You need to be careful, Cass." Turning so I can walk away, a desperate grip on my fingers stops me.

"I'm so sorry." A sob is wrenched from the hunter, and I can almost hear her soul screaming from it. "I'm so, so sorry."

"I know I scare you. No need to be sorry." Feeling all sorts of weird, I try to pull my hand away from her without slicing her skin open.

"It's my fault Helena is dead." Wailing, she yanks on my hand to stop me from pulling away. "It's my fault she was there. I helped her come find you. It should've been me. You should've let me die!"

"What are you talking about?" my snarl stops her sobs, and she stares at me in fear. Luckily, the Archangel does quick work of what is left of the demon or I would leave her there, sliced-open skin or not.

"I stole a car and drove her to you. If I didn't … if I didn't, she'd still be alive." Her voice trembles in a harsh whisper.

"You talk as if you don't know your friend." Raphael moves next to me, placing a paw-sized hand on the woman's narrow shoulder. "Helena would've found them with or without your help. We all should've thought of that."

"Bring her back, Raphael. Please." Tears form tracks on her blood-smeared face, and I see George walking to us from the corner of my eye. "Please bring her back." She keeps repeating it, squeezing my fingers like a lifeline.

"I will. Go help the humans." Raphael nudges her towards George, but she doesn't let go of my hand.

"I'll need all my limbs to help him find her." I meant to sound pissed off, but amusement comes from my mouth.

"Sorry …" mumbling, she uncurls her fingers with effort, her hand dropping listlessly to her side. "Thank you, Eric."

I stare after her, my chest tight when George pulls her under his arm with a firm nod my way. Whispering softly in her ear, he leads her to the rest of the hunters a couple of yards away.

"Not all of them hate just for the sake of hating," Raphael chirps from next to me.

"Keep your preaching for Sunday mass, Archangel." Whirling past him, our shoulders collide, making us both stumble. "Let's find my mate."

"Now that you mention mass, we are in the right place." My neck cracks from how fast I look back at him. His arm is stretched out, a finger pointed at a half-destroyed church right in front of where we are standing.

"Now what?" Changing direction, I step next to him. Closing his eyes for a second, he takes a deep breath and lifts both hands in front of him, palms facing the church. Green and gold power bursts from them, crackling and forming a giant portal in the church grounds.

"Now we visit Purgatory." My mind has no time to register the shock before he sprints at the portal.

I'm right behind him.

Chapter Nine

HELENA

Sand mixed with saliva drips from my gaping mouth when I see a large body burst out of the swirling portal. From the corner of my eye and through my loose clumps of hair, I see the djinn stumble back a step in utter shock. I almost laugh at that, but another body, this one with two sets of horns, comes flying in, his glistening black skin and dark wings standing out harshly in the white sand and bright light.

A sob chokes me, unable to pass my lips. I blink stupidly, praying that I haven't lost my mind to a point where I started imagining things. I mean, is it possible that all I needed to do was remember everything to summon him here? If I knew that, I would've tried harder no matter how terrified I was from bodies pressing me down and my own emotionless face staring at me.

Raphael jumps to his feet first, his wings aggressively flaring to his sides when he spots the still-stunned djinn. It reminds me of the way the holy ass rustled his wings to intimidate me, and a barely audible snicker tumbles from my lips.

Eric is next on his feet, dark wings tucked close to his back, his broad shoulders and double sets of horns intimidation enough. Fists clenched at his sides, blood dripping and sizzling on the sand from his claws digging into his palms, his shoulders bulge, curving inward in rage as he stares daggers at the djinn. My stupid heart thumps excitedly against my ribs. The fact that Eric is here numbs my skull in shock and happiness mixed together. He glances my way and I almost smile, but he turns to look at the djinn, dismissing me. My stomach drops, disappearing somewhere in the sand underneath me.

"Where is she?" Raphael roars at the djinn, taking a threatening step closer.

Shrinking into myself at Eric's dismissal, I slowly crawl back, hoping they'll forget about me. The need to disappear and hide where I can curl up and cry is too overwhelming to ignore. Somewhere in the back of my mind, I'm aware that my behavior is strange and uncalled for, but I can't fight it. The skin on my hands and knees scrapes over the hot sand.

"No angel or demon is allowed in this realm." Snapping out of his shock, the djinn stares down his nose at both of them. "There are consequences for your actions." The evil tilt of his lips curdles the blood in my veins, and I stop my attempt to run and hide.

"That's fine, I'll take my punishment from the one that made us. I asked you where she is?" Undeterred by the threatening tone in the djinn's voice, Raphael snarls at him, shocking the shit out of me with the venom in his voice.

"You better answer him fast or you and your creature will die before you have time to call for help." Eric does that growl deep in his chest that used to annoy me but now sends a flutter in my stomach, but then his words register in my brain and my mouth drops wide open, my jaw unhinging.

"Did you … did you just call me a creature?" stuttering incredulously, I jump to my feet, flipping the loose clumps of hair away from my face with a flourish.

Everyone turns to look at me at the same time, reminding me of all the people wearing my face turning to face me, and I shrink back under their gazes. Raphael moves, but not to come to me. He places himself between me and the djinn, hiding me with the span of his wings. That leaves Eric still standing there frozen, only his chest moving while his Adam's apple bobs in his throat. My broken nails dig in the skin of my palms and I wince. I do look horrible, so it's no wonder he calls me a creature. He must be disgusted by me right now.

His body shimmers, turning my view of him blurry like trying to see the bottom of a river through rushing waters. From one blink to the next, in the spot where the winged Prince of Hell is standing, his green gaze peers at me from a handsome face lacking horns.

"Hel?" rasping my name, his shaking hand reaches for me like he is afraid I will run away or disappear.

"You just called me a creature." Lifting my nose in the air, I glare at him accusingly. Hell yeah, I'll disappear. No woman wants to be called a creature no matter how bad her day has been. Or week. Okay maybe month. I have no idea how long I've been stuck in this endless loop of a clusterfuck the djinn created for me.

All that is beside the point I'm trying to make here.

"Careful, Eric, it may not be Helena." Raphael throws over his shoulder, not looking at us.

Swallowing thickly and with his shaking hand still

reaching for me, Eric smiles and my brain short-circuits at the sight. "Oh, it's Helena angel. There is no doubt."

Raphael jerks around, throwing a couple of quick looks at me but not wanting to take his eyes off the scowling djinn. I glower at him, too. He didn't correct Eric that I'm not a creature. "You are right." Facing the djinn again, he chuckles happily, turning my blood to a boiling point. "No one can fake that pissed off look on her face."

"Seriously?" Throwing my hands in the air, I can't believe what is happening. "You two came here just to insult me? Go back to where you came from, then, because I don't need your help. I was doing just fine on my own." The lie slips from my lips smoothly, while one thought screams on repeat in my head: *I'm not dead, I'm not dead.* I realize that this whole time I was scared shitless of that alone. Swallowing the panic, I take a deep breath, the air whistling through my nose.

"I was almost out of here anyway," the djinn stutters, coughing something from in front of Raphael. "I hope you choke on your tongue, you asshole." Hissing at him while craning my neck to see over Raphael's wings, I startle when I'm jerked forward and wrapped in a crushing embrace.

"Hel." Eric's choked whisper breaks me.

Sobs are muffled in his chest while I claw at his shoulders, trying to bring him closer. If I can get under his skin, nothing will keep me here and away. He will have to carry me no matter where he goes. My body is shaking violently in his arms, but he doesn't notice. His own shoulders are quirking while silent tears drench the side of my face and neck. Eric's tears are the final blow to my sanity. I can almost see it crumbling like a house of cards.

The hard-packed sand under my feet lurches.

The wave is so sudden it sends Eric and me rolling on

the ground. He wraps his arms, one protecting my head, the other my chest, around me like bubble wrap made of hard muscles and mouthwatering scents. We hit something hard that stops our tumbling. I have a second to be confused. Nothing sticks out in this place. Only flat, hot sand flashes through my mind before I'm plucked out of Eric's arms and lifted in the air.

An embarrassing scream echoes around us before fingers as thick as my body is wide curl around me. The second scream dies on my tongue when I face a gigantic version of a familiar face.

"Narsi?"

"I found you again, Mistress." Grinning happily, my now-gargantuan sidekick blinks eyeless sockets in my face.

"Fucking Haltija." Eric snarls. "Put her down right now."

I'm delighted at this moment that no one has given me any water to drink while here. Not that I feel thirsty, but if they had, I would've peed through the already disgusting sack I'm wearing. Narsi looks scary as hell. I remember through a haze seeing him grow in size, but I didn't stay alive long enough to really look at him. Thank goodness I didn't.

"I protected Shadow, Mistress." His deep voice drums in my chest when he places me gently on my feet. Petting my head with one finger, I swat at it and step away, but he is already turning his scary face away from me to look at the djinn. I shiver at the menacing stretch of his lips. "Now, I protect you again."

Eric yanks me to his chest and out of the Trowe's way. With a very girlish squeak that I'll deny until my last breath, I watch my sidekick move swiftly towards the djinn. Eric shoves my face in his chest and I can't see anything anymore.

But I can hear.

First, Narsi informs me happily, "I'll eat his face." The djinn's screams follow, lasting for far too long. My nails dig into Eric's skin, the sound of his heartbeat, which is a little faster than I remember, helping me not lose my shit. Those screams remind me of my own, and that raises the short hairs on my neck.

Then silence.

"We need to get out of here." Eric's voice vibrates on my face through his chest. I turn away from where I know Narsi stands and press my cheek to Eric's hot skin. A frown pulls the skin on my forehead.

"Umm, guys." Blinking doesn't change what I am seeing, or not seeing as is the case. "The portal is gone."

Chapter Ten

RAPHAEL

My skin feels too tight to contain me. Keeping my face expressionless so I don't give my discomfort away, I roll my shoulders. I know it's useless, but I don't dare say it out loud. I have to try, or I'm too scared to think about what the alternative will be.

Lifting my arms up, palms facing out in front of me, I release all the power I can muster. Sparks fly, a portal starts forming, and I hear Helena's excited intake of breath. My bruised heart stutters at the sound, sending a sharp pain jolting through me. The air in front of me swirls in a tiny ball, sweat budding between my shoulder blades and on my lip when I try to expand it. Grinding my teeth, I push harder, my wings snapping open from the effort. With dread, I watch the portal stutter and spit before disappearing in a puff of sparks.

"You almost had it this time," Helena says encouragingly, giving me a slight smile when I look at her.

Giving her a strained smile back, I ignore the scrutinizing look Eric is giving me from over her head. He hasn't let her out of his arms and I don't blame him. I know the feeling too well, how soul-crushing it is for your embrace to be empty. When his eyes squint further, turning into slits, I look away. This is not the time, nor the place for my useless feelings for Zedkiel to drag me down.

"I'm too drained." Staring at the endless stretch of sand in front of me, I stretch my arms over my head. "Opening the portal to get here took a lot of my energy. I will try again … later."

"That's what I wanted to ask," she exclaims, sounding a little too cheerful for having spent time in this realm. "How did you know to find me here?" The sound of feet shuffling through the sand reach me belatedly, and she steps in front of me with her hands on her hips, face tilted up to look at me. "You would've shown up in the tunnel if I was there?"

Uneasiness drills a hole in my gut. "What tunnel?"

Eric glares daggers at me and moves behind her again, wrapping both arms protectively over her shoulders. Rolling her eyes, Helena pets his forearms reassuringly as if calming down a child. If the situation we find ourselves in was different, I would enjoy drilling Lucifer's son about it. As things are, I can't find the humor for the life of me.

"Never mind the tunnel." I don't miss the panicked flash in her gaze.

My skin prickles at that look. The usual liveliness that sparkles there is gone, and what peers at me through the light green depths chills my blood. My eyes snap to Eric's face, unsure if he has noticed the same thing. The muscle jumping in his jaw and the ripple in his arms as he tightens them around her tell me he has.

"I'm just wondering if you would've come no matter where I was." The words are casually spoken, but they do not fool me. She believed she was alone, that we had given up on her.

"I would've opened it no matter where you were." Another lie slips from my lips easily. I have no idea if that's true or not.

Unshed tears shimmering, she gives me a heartfelt smile I do not deserve for all the lies I'm telling her and many more that will follow. Regardless of it all, my mouth lifts at the corners and I reach out to squeeze her shoulder. Eric growls deep in his throat before all the air gushes out of him in a rush.

"Stop growling, Eric." Having elbowed him in the gut, she cranes her neck to glare at him. "I still don't like it. You freaking scare people. Don't you understand that?"

I can't help myself, a snort pushes forward.

Throwing my head back, an honest laugh shakes my body. Helena joins me with a giggle sending a flutter to my chest. No matter how my soul is doomed, this woman can make Death himself crack his expressionless mask. Speaking of which …

"We need to move." Pivoting on my heel, I do a full circle, although nothing has changed the area from my last scanning.

"Where are we anyway?" Slipping out of Eric's arms, she takes his hand. "Heaven? Is that why it's all bright and sunny here? It should be, right? Since the tunnel was all gray with no color …" Her mouth snaps shut audibly when both of us turn to her. "This is not Heaven, is it?"

"No." That one word from Eric makes all the blood drain from her face. "It's not Hell, either." He rushes to assure her, but her expression doesn't change.

She looks at me and a shiver runs up my spine, bursting at the back of my skull and numbing it. It strengthens my resolve that I made the right decision, tightening pain in my chest or not.

"It's Purgatory." I tried and miserably failed to lighten up her expression. "Let us start moving. We can talk on the way." Unable to stand the weight of her gaze, I turn away while my feet sink in the sand with each step.

"How appropriate." Helena is right behind me, dragging a reluctant Eric along with her. "I should've known."

My nostrils flare, my fists clenching at my sides. "How is this appropriate? You shouldn't have been anywhere but where you belong. The human realm."

"This is the ream of the djinn, right? That's what I meant." Grabbing the waistband of my pants, she yanks me back. Stumbling in the shifting sand, I barely manage to stay on my feet. "Slow down, my legs are shorter and I have no intention of running here. Are we in a rush?" At my startled look, she huffs in annoyance. "Not like I wanna be here longer than necessary."

"Purgatory is not a place for any of us. Angel or Demon." Cutting me a side-eyed look, he cups Helena's face in his palm. "It weakens us slowly. Raphael has no time for explanations, obviously. That's why the Haltija didn't have a hard time killing the djinn. I'm guessing it was here as long as you."

Smirking, Helena's face brightens with glee. "Yes, he was. He didn't find anything funny about meeting face to face with Narsi. It made everything worth it."

The Trowe hasn't moved yet, crouching next to the place he disposed of the djinn. We all glance his way, but he just stares in the distance, not paying attention to us. Unsure if that's a good or a bad thing, I continue moving at a slower pace this time.

"So …" Dragging the word out, Helena falls into step

with me. "You feel weaker? Maybe we should sit down so the two of you can rest before we go wherever it is that we are going." Head swiveling from me to Eric, she takes a deep breath and continues talking, "Do we know where we are going? Or did we just pick a random direction? I'm assuming you know what you are doing ..." At my concerned frown, her lips press in a thin line.

"Is everything okay, Helena?" Resisting the urge to pull her into a hug we both desperately need, I force myself to keep my hands to myself. Judging by the death glares he keeps sending my way, I'm sure Eric will not appreciate it either. "You are never this talkative."

"You never know how much you want to talk until you are not allowed to do it." Shoulders slumping, she picks at her nails and avoids our gazes. We look at each other over her head. "If I knew the djinn was weakened, I would've scratched his eyes out before you showed up."

"What happened, Hel?" Eric takes her hand in both of his, pressing it to his chest. "After ..." It takes him a few tries, his throat bobbing before he speaks again. "After you died. Is this where you were the whole time?"

"Yes." Her whispered confirmation sounds so broken it shatters my already shredded heart.

Throwing all the reasons why I should keep walking instead of touching her, I take her other hand the same way Eric has. Her cold, clammy fingers latch onto my hand desperately. He must've heard the fear in her voice too because he offers me a barely perceptible nod.

"Tell us what happened, Helena." At my gentle prodding, her head lifts, showing the tears trickling down her cheeks. "We are here now. You are not alone."

That was all the encouragement she needed. As the words spill out of her mouth along with the tears leaving tracks on her dirt covered face, I keep glancing at my chest, expecting a bleeding wound there. Eric's face flickers a few times, he is fighting for control just as I am. The guilt that was choking me redoubles, and I almost miss what she says. Jerking out of my misery, my eyes snap to Eric. He heard it too.

"There were two of them?" Asking the question that was burning my brain, I search her face.

"Yes?" Her eyes dart around while she tries to remember. "Two of them spoke at one time. I didn't see them then, but since no one else is here, it must've been two djinns." Her focus returns and she narrows her eyes. "You think he is still here?"

The hairs on my neck stand on end the same moment she finishes her question. Pushing her behind my back, I face the threat.

"Yes, he is."

Chapter Eleven

HELENA

"I need my weapon." Frustration and fear twist my insides, and I breathe through my nose so I don't puke all over Raphael's back.

"You'll get it as soon as we get out of here." Eric glides around me, stepping next to Raphael as both of them form a wall of delicious muscle right in my face. "Let us handle it."

They both hide their wings as we are walking, leaving their upper bodies covered in just skin, and in Raphael's case, a collar of what used to be a shirt with a few strands of fabric hanging from it resembling a weird looking necklace. Not even the fact that there is a portal opening ahead of us can squish my hormones from doing a victory dance at the sight. I might be in Purgatory, but my ovaries don't know that, exploding happily when the sun casts shadows in all the nooks and crannies.

Making sure both of them are still staring ahead, I scrub the back of my hand over my mouth in case I just drooled. Alarms blare in my head, freezing my movement halfway when I realize what direction my thoughts are taking me. No wonder they are watching me warily. I seriously have lost my ever-loving mind. Shaking my head to clear it, I lean around Eric, ignoring his hot, sweat-sleeked skin under my palms. My fingers twitch with the need to caress his back.

Poking my head out, my eyes almost fall out of their sockets. The portal opening is nothing like the sparkly circle Raphael opened. It's a gaping black hole expanding before my eyes and ready to devour us all. Heart jumping in my throat, cold sweat plasters my back, making the sack I wear stick to it. I can feel my hands trembling where they are pressed on Eric as the rest of my body shakes violently.

"Oh my God." My lips barely move with my terror-filled whisper. All the air is squeezed out of my lungs.

I almost jump out of my skin when the ground jerks suddenly, my nails leaving bloody scratches on Eric's skin in my attempt to stay standing. Fists the size of large boulders jam deep in the sand, one next to Eric and the other beside Raphael. Looking up forearms the size of tree trunks, I see Narsi's ruffled curls hanging over his scrunched-up, angry face. He is squatting like a runner ready for a sprint with the three of us protected under his body. I'm the only one freaked out. Neither Eric nor Raphael twitch a muscle at this.

"Narsi, keep Helena safe." Eric's deep voice vibrates under my palms.

"I cannot do that, Shadow." Not looking away from the widening portal, he bares his teeth. "I will keep my mistress safe, but I will protect you, as well." I almost laugh at how unhappy he sounds about that last part.

Tiny or humongous, my sidekick always cracks me up.

"Here we go," Raphael mumbles as he poises his body, all the weight shifting to the balls of his feet.

Panic chokes me.

"What do I do? What do I do?" My words trip over each other, coming out in a rush.

Narsi's head comes down to look at me, and I lift my wide eyes to his. I have no weapon, and none of my powers have shown themselves to help me here. Unless I'm planning to scare them with my horrible appearance, I'm just a liability in this fight. The Trowe gives me a smile that curdles the blood in my veins.

Thumps of feet hitting the sand snap my head in their direction. Five djinns resembling the asshole that was laughing at me straighten in a line facing us. None of them carry weapons, but that says nothing about our chances of survival. I've never seen a djinn waving a weapon.

"I will eat their face," Narsi hisses in disgust, quieting the rushing of the blood in my ears.

"Yes!" my exclamation brings the djinn's attention to Eric, and for a moment, I almost believe they can see through him. "Eat them, Narsi. Eat all of them."

Raphael looks at me, the shock evident on his face.

Eric snorts, rolling his shoulders.

"Priorities, angel." Chuckling, he cracks his knuckles, the crunching of his bones setting my teeth on edge. "I think she finally developed a self-preservation skill." Even Raphael brightens, snorting at that comment.

"That's not even funny, asshole." Poking Eric in the ribs, I can't help it when my lips curve up. "Without power or my dagger, Narsi is my weapon."

I swear I can feel the Trowe preening at that. I have every intention of putting him in his place, but that's the moment the djinn move.

Two of them move at Eric and two at Raphael, like they are competing in a synchronized dance, which leaves the one in the middle facing Narsi. Their bronze skin glitters in the harsh glare of the sun, their feet gliding on the sand barely leaving a dent. Eric and Raphael refuse to split up, keeping me hidden behind them, but I know that won't last long. I can feel my skin prickling from the power the djinn is building in their hands. A non-existent wind makes the roped hair over their shoulders dance around like a snake preparing to strike. Narsi hasn't moved either but has remained standing over us like a statue.

"Hold," Raphael mumbles under his breath when I feel Eric stiffen in preparation to move. The muscles on his back relax at the angel's words.

"I should wonder what possessed you to enter this realm, Raphael," the djinn in the middle says, his voice coming from straight ahead of us, unlike the others that are inching on either side.

"That is none of your business," Raphael grinds through clenched teeth. "You shouldn't be here either."

"With Lucifer's son, nonetheless," the djinn continues as if Raphael hasn't spoken.

"We all know why we are here," Eric growls, his shoulders curving inward aggressively. "Let's not waste time on chatter, huh?"

Tsking as if disappointed, the djinn sighs. "Risking all this for a girl that should not exist. Such a shame. Show yourself, girl, no reason to hide."

"Stay back, Helena." My hackles rise when Eric speaks over his shoulder, but I stay rooted in the sand, my anxiety making me mute.

"For a mighty being, hiding is the last thing I expected." He keeps mocking me, and anger surges through me.

"I'm just here for the tan dude. I heard the weather is nice around these parts this time of the year." Slapping a hand over my mouth, I stop any other crap that was about to spill from it.

"You dare mock me!" His snarl is the signal the rest of the djinn need.

Strong winds slam at Eric, forcing him to slide back, his feet digging deep in the sand until they are buried to his ankles. He whirls around, wings bursting and double horns growing as he throws himself at the two djinns on his left. Another wave hits from the other side, the air so dense it's like a brick wall ramming in my face, and Raphael slides his body back, leaning forward at an angle in his hopes to stay standing. As soon as the onslaught stops, his wings open, and he jumps the two djinns on his right.

With dread, I lower my arms where I have them curled over my head to protect my eyes from the sand pummeling my skin. Gulping down my fear, I look straight at the djinn in front of me. A smile has never been so terrifying as the one that graces his perfect face.

"There you are," he purrs.

Chapter Twelve

HELENA

Flashes of memories are trying to double me over and I can't breathe. The tunnel repeating over and over, a face looking like the one staring at me with empty violet eyes chuckling while I am slowly losing my mind. I'll never admit it to anyone, not even to Eric, but I begged silently in my head for the asshole to just kill me. I fought to remember only so that I'm not petrified, so I don't feel alone. If I remember just one person who cares about me, I will have something to hold onto.

And it's all their fault.

The djinn.

Hot burning rage clears my airways and I suck in a lungful of hot air. Sand sticks to my lips and gets on my tongue, but I ignore it. Eric's words that everyone weakens in this realm swirl in the front of my mind. If that's the case, then how did I manage to remember? How did I fight against whatever fresh hell these creatures created in hopes of breaking me?

My skin feels tight, all the emotions that are crippling

me bubbling over. As I stare in the empty depths of those violet eyes, everything comes rushing in like a tsunami hitting a peaceful shore. A high-pitched sound whistles in my ears, drowning out the echoes of fighting and the slaps of flesh hitting flesh, the grunts and growls all disappearing in a never-ending even tone.

The perfect face in front of me gets distorted by a line forming between two perfectly-shaped eyebrows. That terrifying smile slips from his lips, an emotionless mask replacing it. I watch him dispassionately as his body leans slightly forward like he can't believe what he is seeing. I have no idea how I look, but I welcome the calm that washes over me with one realization.

Anything is better than being afraid.

Even death.

The djinn's eyes widen incredulously as my smile grows. Still standing in the shadow Narsi's body is casting over me, I jut my hip to the side, placing my hand on it. Cocking my head, I scan the djinn from head to toe, pulling a face like I find him lacking.

"Here I am, asshole." I can't recognize the throaty purr in my voice. "What are you going to do about it?"

"Now, you cease to exist," the djinn spits at me, his jaw clenching.

My body hits Narsi's forearm, jarring my bones when I jump to grab it a second before the djinn's power sends a punishing wave of dense air my way. Clinging to my sidekick like a koala, my fingers grapple at his skin so I don't fly off him. The strength of the wind doubles, but Narsi doesn't move an inch as he stands like an ominous mountain looming over all of us. The longer it goes on, the harder it is for me to hang on. Then the Trowe lifts his arm —the one I'm not holding onto like a Velcro—and pulls it back. The next thing I know, his fist slams on top of the djinn's head, burying him in the sand like a nail under a nail gun. The entire body disappears and the wind abruptly stops. I slide down his forearm listlessly, all my strength deserting me. My knees buckle and I crumble next to his fist, leaning my head on it. It takes everything in me to not lose my grip on Narsi.

"Thank you." Petting him halfheartedly, I shift to the side to see how the others are doing.

The sound hasn't returned to my ears, so I watch Eric and Raphael fighting, their movement fast and precise on either side of us. The moment one of the djinns is able to step away from their flying fists and kicks, they blast them with those damn winds and send them tumbling through the air, only for Eric and Raphael to return a moment later with a renewed viciousness. As I pant to catch my breath, one thing becomes very clear. Nothing changes. We are not winning, but not losing either. Opening my mouth to ask Narsi why he is not helping, a shrill scream is ripped from my chest when my head is yanked back by a fistful of my hair.

"You stupid girl," the djinn snarls in my ear, bending my head back so much I'm worried my neck will snap if he keeps pulling.

Ramming my fist in his face, I hear the satisfying crunch of the bone when his nose breaks. Releasing my hair, he stumbles back away from me, eyes bulging in shock while blood ruins his perfect face by gushing over his mouth and chin. His hair is covered in sand, and the bronzed skin is dusty, dimming his glow. I expect my hand to hurt from the strong impact, but I feel nothing. Turning to face him, I brace a hand on Narsi's forearm and pivot on one foot, putting all the strength on the spin of my hips while executing a perfect kick to his head. Neck bending in an odd angle, his body drops on the sand in a heap, the shocked expression frozen on his blood-covered face.

"I think the djinn fight with their power so much that an old-fashioned kick in the head is a surprise," I tell no one in particular, still staring at the dead djinn.

"He will rise again, mistress." Not expecting an answer, my head jerks up to look at Narsi.

"Eat him, then." I'm aware that this is not typical behavior for me, but nothing so far is exactly normal in this realm. "You should help Eric and Raphael as well."

"They do not need it." Deep voice rumbling, Narsi snatches the djinn and I look away so I don't see him eating it. The queasiness I usually feel at the thought is missing, too.

Eric drops on one knee and the air punches my throat. I'm running before a thought is formed in my mind. Jumping in the air as soon as I'm near enough, I curl my knees and jam all my weight into the djinn's back. The rage turns my vision red, my banshee scream echoing around us. I don't stop punching the back of his head until strong arms wrap around me like metal bands restricting my movement.

"Hel." Eric's voice is raspy like he's been yelling my name for a while.

At the sound of his voice, I go limp, sliding my legs down his body and gasping for air. He pulls me closer, tightening his arms and burying his face in my neck. My feet hang a foot off the ground, but he holds me like I weigh nothing.

"He is dead, Hel. It's okay. It's okay," repeating it over and over in a raspy whisper, he holds me like that until my heartbeat evens out, and I'm breathing properly.

When the blurriness clears from my vision, I see

Raphael standing right in front of me, his face tortured and eyes swimming in unshed tears. Without a thought, I try to reach for him with my twitching hand, but I'm unable to move from Eric's tight hold. The Archangel comes despite that. Pressing me between himself and Eric, he leans his forehead on my other shoulder. Eric doesn't protest or growl, for which I'm grateful. I feel like I'm unraveling at the seams and Raphael's calm presence soothes me like nothing else.

"We need to get out of here before I lose myself." Voicing some of my fears, I feel both of them stiffen. "Do we know a way out?"

"I'll feel the shift in the air where the invisible portals are. We need to get going." Raphael tries to pull away, but the strangled sound coming from me stops him.

"We will go, just stay where you are." Swallowing my pride, I tangle my fingers in the fabric on the side of his pants so he can't escape. "Just a bit longer."

I feel him nod once where his head is still on my shoulder, and I sag deeper between their quiet strength and protection. I'm not sure if Eric hears his heartbreaking whisper when he says, "Thank you."

Chapter Thirteen

HELENA

"One good thing about this place is that we don't need to drink or eat." I can't stop myself from rambling. I tried.

"True." The ever-so-helpful Eric keeps giving me one-word answers.

"It would've been very awkward even if we had things to eat or drink, you know." My hand flops like a fish out of water in his face. "Imagine if I had to pee." Raphael makes a strangled sound, but I ignore him since he stopped answering me a while ago. "Awkward!"

"Very awkward, Hel." Eric's head bobs up and down, but he is not looking at me. He keeps scanning the area we are passing.

"Why do I get the feeling I'm bothering the two of you?" Glowering at both of them in turn, I stop walking. "First"—I stick one finger in the air for emphasis— "you have nothing better to do here but talk to me." Another finger joins the first one. "Second, stop staring because the view hasn't changed at ALL. Not even one damn grain of sand looks different." One more finger goes up, and I curl the other two down, flipping both of them off. "Third, this is for acting like I'm an idiot indulging me with small talk."

Both of them watch me like I've grown a second head before scaring the shit out of me when they roar with laughter. I stare daggers at the top of their heads when they double over, slapping their thighs. I honestly can't see how what I say is funny. They are such jerks. My eyes flick back when Narsi takes a step closer. My sidekick moves once every minute or two, that way his pace matches ours as we walk.

"I don't like it when you get that look on your face, Helena." Raphael makes an effort to stop laughing, but a few more chuckles come out of him.

"It means trouble." Eric nods at the Archangel, backing up his ridiculous claims.

"I have no idea what look you are talking about." Sniffing promptly, I pivot on my foot and stomp away. "Feel free to change the subject all you want. I still think it'll be awkward if I have to pee."

"We agree with the merit of that wisdom," Raphael chirps, unable to hide his amusement.

Now that both of them are behind me, my smile slips and I blow a silent breath out. Seeing them with anguish in their eyes and tortured looks on their faces every time they look at me is like someone twisting a dagger in my chest. If I have to act like a fool to make it go away, so be it. One of us being broken is enough. I bought a front-row ticket for that one, so they don't need to suffer for my stupidities.

"You still haven't felt any shift in the air?" Turning to look at them with a smile plastered on my face, I walk backward.

"Not yet." A shadow passes over Raphael's gaze, but he

looks away from me too fast to be sure. "It must be here somewhere. We've been walking for some time."

"I didn't thank you for coming for me," blurting it out, I press my mouth shut.

I'm not sure why I say it now. It may be the severe look on his face that chases away his smile. Or it is eating me long enough inside that it has to come out. Since I can't take the words back, I make sure the Archangel sees my gratitude on my face and hears it in my voice.

"Although I don't know my mother and I'll never get a chance to meet her ... I'll be grateful to her until the end of my days for leaving you to watch over me." My voice cuts off, emotions clogging my throat while I blink away the tears threatening to spill out.

Raphael stops dead in his tracks. Panic bubbles in my chest when his face drains of all color, but it changes fast enough that I'm left staring at the Archangel with my mouth hanging open. From shock to guilt, pain to fear ... they all pass his features, flicking from one to the next until shame reddens his face and he drops on his knees in front of me bowing his head.

My heart jumps at the sight, almost punching a hole through my chest. I might not know many things, but having an Archangel bowing at your feet can't be an everyday thing. Or a good one for that matter.

"I have failed her, Helena." Never have I thought I'd hear the calm and levelheaded, always kind Raphael sound so destroyed. "I have failed you both." His shoulders tremble as he grabs fistfuls of sand.

"What are you talking about?" Dropping on my knees in front of him, I yank on his shoulders so he can look up. "You found me when I had no idea where I was or if I was even alive."

"She speaks the truth, Archangel." Eric looms over us, casting us under a shade with his body. "I never would've found her without you. I was so lost in my grief I would've been locked in the pits of Hell eventually. I still might end up there for what I've done."

"What?" Squinting up at him, his grim expression tightens my stomach, but Raphael is still kneeling. "Never mind, we will talk about you later. Raphael, please. Please get up. You saved me. Do you hear me?" Shaking him to bring some sense into his head, he finally looks at me through glistening lashes.

"I have not saved you yet." His nostrils flare. "You shouldn't even be here. If I stayed with you ... if I didn't leave ..."

"If you didn't, the same thing would've happened, only that way you would've blamed yourself even more." I'm not psychic, but I know it's the truth as I say it.

"We could've kept your power under control. Between Satanael and me, you would've survived it." I know that stubborn look on his face. I've seen it in the mirror too many times.

No matter what I say to him, he will keep blaming himself for what happened. The Archangel might be stubborn, willing to carry the guilt like an anvil around his neck, but he doesn't skim the surface of how headstrong Helena can be. I'm not going to convince him with words, but I'm going to kick his ass back in line by showing him with actions. Acting on instinct, I throw my hands around his neck, squeezing the shit out of him when he tries to jerk away.

"That's fine. Thank you anyway for coming for me, and for bringing monster boy with you." When he stops squirming, I relax my death grip on his neck.

Reluctantly, he places his hands on my back but barely touches me, while at the same second he stiffens. Jolting up on his knees, he pulls me along with him even with me still hanging on his neck, plastering myself to his chest. Thick fingers wrap around my arms, lifting me off the Archangel, and Eric places me gently on my feet with a low growl in his throat. I'm confused as hell until Raphael speaks.

"A portal is near."

Chapter Fourteen

ERIC

I take up the rear, placing Helena between myself and the Archangel. There is something going on with him, and the fact I don't notice it until we come here tells me how far gone in my fury I'd been after losing Helena.

My eyes drift to her body covered in a shapeless, hole-ridden cloth. It hangs over her shoulders to her knees, covering most of her. But I held her in my arms, barely holding onto my control when I felt her bones sticking out. Her arms and legs are covered in dirt and dried blood, the silky golden hair matted with no shine in it. Clamping my mouth shut tight so I don't release the growl building in my chest, I keep a couple feet of distance between us. I want nothing more than to have her tucked under my arm where I can maintain contact with her skin, but right now, I know she won't appreciate my clinginess.

Something is wrong.

With my mate, with the Archangel ... with this whole damn realm. Until I figure it out, I'll keep an eye on everyone from the sidelines. The ground trembles under my feet, the Haltija moving closer to us again. There is something wrong with him, too. My wings twitch in agitation. The fucking djinn make sure I'll chase them to the ends of the world and pick them off one by one if it's the last thing I do.

Raphael stops, his arm shooting out to hold us back. My eyes narrow as I watch him tilt his head this way and that like he is listening for something. Turning my face to the side while still keeping him in my line of sight, I strain my ears to see if there is a sound. Apart from our heartbeats and our breathing, nothing else can be heard.

"We are very close." Looking over his shoulder, Raphael locks his golden eyes on mine. There is no indication on his face that he is happy to find our way out of here.

"Do we know where the portal leads?" I don't raise my voice but I know he can hear me.

"No." His mouth mashes together in a grim line. Ah, so that's what has him stiff this whole time.

"What does that mean?" Helena's face turns from me to Raphael. "We can end up in that black hole the djinn opened?"

"No," Raphael rushes to assure her, and I squint at him. "Only djinn can open a portal to their own realm. The ones popping in and out of existence in Purgatory lead to Heaven or Hell."

"Is that why you couldn't open the one to the human realm?" My mate narrows her eyes in suspicion, seeing right through the Archangel's bullshit story from earlier.

"My power is almost nonexistent in this realm, Helena." Looking pained, Raphael stares at his feet. "Souls ending up in purgatory shouldn't be from Heaven, or from Hell." After one quick glance my way, he continues talking to his feet. "You haven't seen anyone else because they all live in their own personal torment and fear. None of them made a choice to pick a side. Neither light nor darkness."

"Is that why I ended up here? Because I refused to choose?" Helena's fingers twist in the shapeless sack as she strangles the life out of it. My chest feels tight, and I can't stop the snarl from escaping.

She gives me a small smile that flutters my gut.

"Not true." The conviction in Raphael's voice calms me down, if only just a little. "I'm not yet sure why you are here, but it was the only logical place." At my raised eyebrow, Raphael scowls at me. "I believe it was the only place for a being like you because otherwise, you'd have to be split in a few pieces. No one can do that, and nothing has that power. You are made half of Heaven, half of Hell, and you shun them both in your own way. But you still made a choice." Gracing her with a gentle smile I've seen him offer her often—like a parent guiding a child—pride shines for the first time since he found me in the destroyed Atlanta. "You chose humanity. With all its virtues and its vices. Nothing in existence can begrudge you that. Nothing!"

I might get annoyed by the fucker, but I'm grateful to him at this moment when I see Helena's shoulders relax and her entire posture change into one I know too well. I give him a nod that he reluctantly returns.

"I always pay my debts, Archangel."

"This is not a debt you need to pay, Shadow." I can tell I insulted him by the glare he sends me without hearing him call me by my true name.

I smirk at him.

"It's here."

Raphael whirls around. I instinctively brace for an

attack, but when nothing happens in a long moment, my feet inch closer to Helena. Pride warms my chest that she stands calm with her chin up, waiting on whatever happens. We watch the Archangel lift both arms pausing for something. Not knowing what he is doing, I step ahead of my mate, placing her slightly at my back without being too obvious about it. Or I think I'm not until the breath is stuck in my lungs. I swallow the sound in hopes I don't grunt when she elbows me in the kidneys.

In a swift movement like trying to catch a fish with his bare hands, Raphael plunges both arms in front of him. The air ripples around them, distorting the view before a slight shimmer appears. Both Helena and I move closer to him when his muscles bulge, telling us he is struggling to hold it. Whether keeping it here or opening it, I'm not sure. Unwilling to let our chance pass to get out of here, I step next to him.

"What do you need from me?" His body jerks forward, and I grab hold of his arm.

"I don't have enough strength to fully open it." Hissing through his teeth from the effort, I watch him debate in his mind. "If you can lend me some power, we might have it wide enough and open long enough for all of us to go through."

My head turns to the Haltija at his words. I'm not sure giving all my power can open the portal that wide if the Archangel is struggling with it. My mouth parts in surprise when the damn thing grins at me and, with a ripple of air, shrinks to his standard size before bolting and tangling around Helena's legs.

"Narsi!" Her excited shout has even Raphael's attention, and I will live the rest of my days happy when I hear the Archangel curse up a storm.

"Now you can have everything you need." With a chuckle, I slap him on the back before gripping his shoulders. His strangled laugh widens my grin.

"Whenever you are ready." Raphael braces his feet, biceps straining against the portal. Helena comes next to me, the damn grinning Haltija hanging happily like a child on her hip.

With a shake of my head, I brace my own feet and push everything I have at the Archangel. Shadows start snaking out of me, hissing and sizzling like water drops over a fire. My skin tightens from the discomfort, but I clench my jaw when I hear Raphael grunting in pain. The portal spreads, solidifying in front of us. Arms shaking, I clutch at Raphael's shoulders, my claws embedding themselves in his skin.

"Helena, go." The words are wrenched out of the Archangel's chest.

Eyes narrowed, my mate looks from me to Raphael and back. My gut drops at my feet when I see determination setting on her soot-smudged face. Even the Haltija scans us with a calculating expression on his eyeless face.

"We all go."

Before my brain registers her words, I feel her slam her body at my back. Being braced to push forward only eases her intention, and I hit Raphael with a lot more force than possible. The Archangel screams when half of his body passes through the portal, but there is no turning back now.

"Eric push, it's killing him!"

Helena's frantic scream freezes the blood in me, and I redouble my efforts. Dread like acid burns a hole in my chest from Raphael's roars. My mate's weight on my back disappears for just a moment before all air is punched out of me when she slams with all she's got one more time. My skin feels like its passing through a shredder as my body goes through the portal following Raphael. A roar rips from my throat that I can't hold back. It spits us on the other side, and I can feel Helena's weight still on my body. Fear numbs my brain.

She didn't make a sound.

Chapter Fifteen

HELENA

Limbs trembling, I push shakily off Eric. My eyes search for signs that he and Raphael are alive, their roars of pain still ringing in my ears. I want to squeeze them shut, unwilling to see that in their attempt to save me, they've given their own lives. Whatever fates have been using us for their amusement can't be that cruel. A muffled grunt makes me scramble faster to remove my weight from Eric's back.

Wings twitching, Eric rolls off Raphael, landing on his side with a thump. His arm slides under him as he tries to lift himself up, but he buckles a second later, dropping his head in the dirt. Raphael hasn't moved. He's sprawled face down, wings awkwardly half-flared around him. Narsi is crawling opposite me, sniffing the Archangel with a scrunched-up face.

Panic builds in me, choking the air in my shriveling chest.

"Hel?" Eric groans, lashes fluttering before he goes still.

A shrill scream pierces the air, the echoes making the sound surround us from every side. My heart kicks at my ribs, my head snapping up for the first time to see where we ended up. Tall trees reach for the oppressive, gloomy skies while a red moon glares at us from right above our heads. Anticipation promising violence hangs heavy, thickening the air forcing its way into my lungs.

I almost jump out of my skin when a harsh wind whistles through the wide tree trunks, swaying the treetops ominously and snapping their branches. Whispers can be heard when it picks the clumps of my hair up and flings it around my face. A shiver washes up and down my spine, my skin prickling and raising goosebumps over my arms and legs. Voices murmuring words I can't catch sound like they are coming from graves and reaching for my soul. Another shiver racks me. I fold my arms over my middle and curl into a ball with my forehead pressed to my knees.

The burning sensation from before in the portal numbs from the terror clogging my throat. It felt like someone was peeling the skin off my shoulders when I passed through, but the sounds coming from Eric and Raphael didn't give me much time to think of my own pain. Now, fear shoves it to the back of my mind. It can't be that bad if I'm still conscious, especially since the two of them are still out cold.

As suddenly as they start, the wind and the whispers stop, plunging everything in a calm silence I almost think I imagine it all. With a loud thwack, a branch separates from a tree somewhere on my side and thumps on the forest floor in sync with the punch of my heart in my throat. Frantic urgency propels me to my feet. The portal spit us out in a clearing wide enough to fit a small house in it and, after the warm welcome I just witnessed, I know nothing good can come from staying here like sitting ducks.

Can the djinn find us here?

Rushing around Eric, I debate how to grab him for a

second before crouching next to him and flipping him on his stomach. I might turn his skin into mincemeat by dragging him like this but at least I'm not going to break his wings. My gaze darts over his broad shoulders and arms as wide as my thighs. Why couldn't he have stayed in his human form?

"Because fate is a bitch, Hel. That's why."

Murmuring breathlessly, I snake my hands under his arms. Bracing my legs, I pull.

My face turns red, chest tight from the air I'm holding, and I can feel my heartbeat in my temples. Legs quacking with effort, thighs spasming, I yank with all I've got. His upper body lifts off the ground, scraping over the dusty floor for one glorious moment before my foot slips. Pitching back, my hands lose their grip as my fingers slide off his sweat-sleeked skin. With a girly squeak and my arms flopping in circles like a baby bird learning to fly, I land on my ass, jarring my teeth as all the air punches out of me. Eric's head hits the dirt with a loud thump at the same time.

"Oomph …" Fighting for air, I shake my head to clear the lightheadedness.

Narsi snickers.

"There is nothing funny, you little shit." Gasping for air I glare at him over Eric and Raphael. He spins in a circle while giggling like a nut job. "I'm glad I can entertain you." Lifting on my knees and wincing with each movement, I rub my butt cheeks while considering both men again.

Although the same height, Raphael looks smaller beside Eric's bulky frame. Rethinking my strategy, I shuffle closer to the Archangel on my knees while catching my breath. When I'm level with his head, I squat in front of him, nestling his underarms at my elbows. Wiggling my ass, I widen my feet, take a deep breath that I hold in, and I yank.

I almost shout in victory when my legs straighten and Raphael's body lifts off the ground, his wings draping over him like a blanket made of feathers.

"Narsi," I barely manage to push the words through my teeth. "Stay with Eric."

Even after endless loops in that damn tunnel, my poor bare feet still sting when I move without lifting them, one painful step after another. Raphael's head bumps in my pelvis when I sway and stagger, the tops of his thighs and his shins forming a line in the packed dirt. Huffing, grunting, and sweating bullets, I almost cry out in happiness when the dark shadows of the trees hide the red glare of the moon.

After maneuvering the Archangel around tree trunks, fallen branches, and anything else in my way, I drop him on the ground by a tree and plop down next to him exhausted. I didn't think this through. Jaw clenched and teeth grinding, I cradle one foot in my lap while plucking sticks and rocks that are stabbing me out of my skin. The shredded skin gapes open, blood smearing over the black soles. Sore or not, I don't want to leave Eric out in the open for too long, so I stand up, catching myself on a tree so I don't topple over when everything around me spins like a carousel.

"No rest for the wicked." I'm glad no one can hear me right now because I don't sound badass at all. I sound pained, drained, and pathetic.

With one last glance at Raphael nestled between the thick, gnarled roots of a tree, I head back. Now that I'm not depriving my lungs of oxygen from the weight I'm dragging, my urgency returns. It's almost like the air is heating up and burning my skin. A fleeting thought ping pongs through my head. *Have I lost all my powers?* Apart from the strange feeling from before—between the reoccurring nightmare the djinn created—I don't feel anything at all. Pushing off the tree trunks, I finally reach the clearing completely lost in my thoughts.

Narsi lifts his head from Eric's wing he is sniffing as I exit the tree line. My shoulders straighten, my spine straightening now that I know someone is watching me. Not that the Trowe will judge me if I collapse next to Eric. I don't think anything I do can make him think less of me. I mean, I've kicked him inside Lucifer's fireplace for God's sake and here he is, happy as a pig in mud just to be around me. The annoyance that still lingers from earlier when he laughed at me evaporates at that thought.

"Narsi, can you help me drag big boy out of the open?" My muscles spasm just looking at Eric's broad back.

"Yes, Mistress." He hisses happily doing that twirled circle again. "I'll help drag Shadow."

"You're not going to hurt him, are you?" Narrowing my eyes at him, I watch him squirm.

"No." His tiny shoulders slump in defeat and I almost laugh. Eric will strangle him if he hears him.

A stronger gust of wind comes out of nowhere, the closest trees almost bending in half from it. With a strangled scream, I throw myself over Eric, and Narsi's slight weight thumps on my back. His tiny fingers pinch the skin on my arms where he holds on for dear life the same way my nails dig into Eric so I don't fly off him. Unchanged whispers fill my ears, only this time they are more urgent and they freeze the blood in my veins. My bones rattle when we slide harshly on the ground for one long, excruciating moment before everything abruptly stops. I still cling to Eric, my fingers like claws. No matter how hard I try I can't uncurl them to lift myself off him.

"We have to go, Mistress." Narsi jumps off my back.

"Now, you're in a rush?" Panting, I force my eyes open. I have no idea when I closed them.

With strength I didn't know he possessed, Narsi pulls me off Eric. Stunned, I gape at him as he pulls me to my feet with a single yank on my arm. All the questions swirling in my head disappear when I see his worry-filled gaze eyeing the trees to the right even as he scrambles to grab Eric's arm. Springing into motion, I take hold of the other arm and, without waiting, we both pull. Eric's body slides in the dirt for a foot before I trip over my own feet and almost faceplant next to him, only catching myself with my palms when they slap on the ground. Narsi keeps yanking, dragging him sideways without stopping.

"Let me hold both arms and you just help with his weight."

Whatever scared the Trowe gives me enough strength to grab both of Eric's arms and lift him high enough to be able to pull him along. Narsi slides under his chest, pressing his shoulders under Eric's chest. Between both of us we are able to move faster this way.

Reaching the tree line, my foot twists awkwardly in a dip on the forest floor. I don't have time to make a sound when gravity takes hold, making me bite my tongue when the back of my head hits the ground. My grip on Eric is gone and dark spots dance in front of my eyes. Just as I think I'm about to faint, I suck in air to fill my starving lungs. Weight presses over my lower body and I look down.

The ugly sack I'm wearing is bunched up at my waist. Eric's head is nestled between my thighs, his face pressed firmly at my core. Both his arms trap my legs, pinning me under him. Heat that I have no right to feel right now sends flutters through my stomach, my core throbbing and clenching at the sight. I stare at his tousled hair and twisting horns for a few breaths until a muffled sound reaches my ears.

"Oh, my god. Narsi!" Wiggling and twisting like an eel, I jerk my hips up, ignoring Eric's face rubbing over all the places he shouldn't be rubbing while unconscious. I lift him enough for Narsi to crawl out from under him and almost laugh when the Trowe jumps out hissing at him before giving his ribs a halfhearted kick.

"Stupid Shadow." He bares his yellow teeth.

"Little help here, Narsi."

Pretending that I'm breathless instead of trying hard not to laugh, I'm glad when he yanks Eric off me. Ignoring my body that is one big, sore bruise at this point, I jump up. Together, we pull Eric further inside the cover of the trees. Narsi is still glaring at the top of Eric's head, and I am still wincing and limping on one leg. We only reach the second row of trees, Eric's feet only disappearing a couple feet from view before the blood drains from my face.

Narsi's head snaps in my direction before the first sound screams around us.

Chapter Sixteen

HELENA

Sweat drenches the sack I wear, making it stick it to my skin. My choked gasps are partly from dragging Eric's weight and partly from the fear clawing at my throat. Now that he and Raphael are tucked under the huge tree, their bodies covered with the broken branches I haul from around it, I twist my shaky hands.

Screams.

The sounds were brain-numbing. I've heard all sorts of sounds indicating pain and fear—even terror—in my life-time. Nothing like the gut-wrenching screams that assault my ears as soon as all of us are under the protection of the forest. Accompanying them are hoots, short bursts of victory shouts, and laughter. The longer I stand here with my heart galloping like a frightened rabbit against my chest, the clearer they become.

Eyes darting around, every shadow that flickers sends a jolt of something like a freefall sensation in my stomach. Narsi is crouched between the gnarled roots, hands resting on the ground between his feet with his head canted to the side.

"Narsi?" My shaky breath shudders through numb lips, the heartbeat in my throat making it difficult to speak.

The Trowe tilts his face up with a wary expression on his wrinkled face. A dim light flashes over his features, scrunching my forehead in confusion, but another scream erases it and I almost jump out of my skin. Swallowing the panic that makes me want to curl up in a ball and press my hands over my ears, I grind my teeth. I have to know what's going on. If nothing else, at least I'll know what I'm afraid of. At the moment, my mind is creating all sorts of insane scenarios and I'll have a heart attack sooner than anyone can kill me. My fingers twitch, hands desperate for my dagger clenching and grasping air.

"Narsi, stay here and protect them." Blowing a steadying breath through pursed lips, I ignore the voice in my head telling me how stupid this idea is. "I'll be right back."

Forcing my limbs to move, I shuffle woodenly away from the tree. I haven't taken five steps when something brushes over the exposed skin on my shin. The terrified scream that almost announces where I am gets lodged in my throat when I see Narsi's grinning face looking up at me. The relief that it's not something that will kill me makes me lightheaded and I stagger on my feet, catching myself at the last minute on the nearest tree.

"I told you to stay back," I spit when I can finally speak, anger evident in my tone.

He has the decency to pout.

"Go back and protect them. I'll be right back. Anything can attack and kill them while they are unconscious." His eyeless sockets train on my face as he considers me for a long moment, then he whirls in annoyance and scutters back to Eric and Raphael.

Releasing the breath I'm holding, I scrub my hands over my face, probably smudging all the crap stuck to my skin even more. My toes wiggle between leaves and twigs as I pick my way through the forest, heading in the direction of the screams instead of running away from them.

The sound of my breathing is too loud in my ears, the looming trees zipping by me as I dart from one to the next, the bark scraping the shit out of my hands in the process. Fear must be muddling my brain and causing me to misjudge the speed I'm going, along with the distance between trees. Or maybe I just forgot how to walk. Sore, I move further away from everyone, forgetting about my throbbing ankle since my life is precariously hanging on the line. I glance back often to ensure Narsi hasn't ditched Eric and Raphael to come and hang with me again, something I definitely wouldn't put past him.

"This must be Hell." Murmuring under my breath just to fill the silence, I scan the gaps between tree trunks.

From my first glance after I passed through the portal, that fact was burned in my mind. Hell is the only place where I've seen trees like these and nature untouched by human hands. *Not that you know what Heaven looks like,* a snide voice sneers in my head but I push it away. I believed Archangel Michael wanted to kill me before I learned the one I call a holy ass was actually a djinn disguised as the mighty angel.

Heaven is the last place I want to be.

Leaning over a wide trunk, I hold my breath as I search the darkness for any movement. The screams are closer but

I'm still alone here. Straightening, I press my back on a tree. My nostrils flare, the air whistling through them as my mind races. If this is Hell why did Eric drop unconscious as soon as he stepped through the portal. To make things worse, how on earth did Raphael enter then? Because as far as I know, Fallen or demons can't just waltz into Heaven, so I assume it is the same for Angels in hell.

The tree supports my weight as I catch my breath. No matter where we are, I just hope it's not inside the pitch-black hole where the djinn is. I still don't understand how I managed to kick the one so hard I almost ripped his head off in Purgatory. No matter how much weaker they are there, it still took all my uncontrollable power to defeat them back home.

A crunch of a twig breaking is like a bomb going off around me.

My eyes snap open, even though I have no idea when they closed. Widening them, I try to see everywhere all at once. Tiny flashes of light spark in different areas as I walk, like fireflies blinking in and out of existence. Somehow, I ignored them. Now two of them flicker from the leaves and trees in front of me no matter where I look, like they can predict where my eyes will land next. I don't dare breathe, pressing to the trunk in hopes whoever it is moves away without seeing me.

"You think they saw us running away?" a husky guttural voice huffs out a whisper way too close for my comfort.

"They would've been on top of us if they did," another, this one deeper and more masculine, answers with an unmistakable growl. "They are killing everything in their path and letting no one escape."

"They'll come for us." The first voice whimpers and my

stomach clenches at the sound because I can relate to the fear in it. "If no one escapes, they'll come."

"If Satanael doesn't find us first." When the second voice spits my father's name in disgust, my ears perk up. *It is Hell!* the voice in my head bellows in victory. "I heard madness took his mind and he is slaughtering friend and foe." The sound of clothing rustling comes from just behind my tree. "Let me see. You are hurt."

"It's nothing. It'll heal," the husky voice whispers. "I would rather die staring Satanael in the eyes than letting those murderers do it after invading my home."

Djinn. They must be talking about djinn. The bastards have invaded Hell and started killing everyone here. My fingers dig into the bark of the tree, shavings of it stabbing under my nails and filling them up. The husky voice whimpers a second before a bright light like a lightning strike splits the darkness, bringing the forest around me to life. With a shriek that pebbles my skin and sends a shiver rolling down my spine, the two demons race past me without sparing me a glance. A man and a woman holding hands bolt too, disappearing through the trees but thankfully not in the direction of Eric and Raphael. With crippling dread, I slide sideways on the tree trunk and poke my head out just enough for one of my eyes to see what's behind me. I hope it's just one djinn because I'm not sure I'll survive that fight right now.

My mouth drops open, my jaw hitting my chest as bright spots dance in the corners of my eyes. Right in front of me, in the middle of a dark, gloomy forest in Hell, is not a djinn as I first think. No, that will make everything too easy. Instead of one of my archenemies, it's another being, his feet planted shoulder width apart while he lifts a bright sword that crackles with power in the air. One that cannot possibly be here.

An angel stabs his sword towards the sky and the night splits with blinding light as one of the snaking bolts zaps my hand. With a yelp, I press my back on the tree and cradle it to my chest.

Chapter Seventeen

RAPHAEL

The stench of leaves and dry soil fills my nostrils. With a groan, I lift my head up only for it to thump uselessly on the ground. Weight is pressing on me, sharp things poking uncomfortably at my wings and back. Like a newborn babe, I manage to breathe even though dust fills my lungs with each inhale. Why do I feel like I have fought a year-long battle? My mind is muddled, each thought moving through a sludge.

Shoulders stiffening, I instantly become alert when the shuffling of leaves reaches my ears. Too low murmuring, like an insistent buzzing, continues for a moment before silence presses like a thick blanket over me. Everything comes in a rush, the fight, the portal, and the excruciating pain when I was pushed out of Purgatory. Darkness follows.

With a groan, I slide my hands under my chest, rocks digging into my palms as I push myself up on my hands and knees. The weight slides off my back, tugging painfully on my limp wings. I can't summon the energy to pull them in and spare myself the agony. Shaking my head, I look around to see the thick, leaf-ridden branches that fell off me. My hand grazes warm skin and with a jolt, I realize Eric is pressed next to me in his other form, horns twisted between the branches still covering his body.

Shifting around fast, I search for Helena, pitching sideways. I barely catch myself before I hit the large trunk of the tree where we are nestled. My eyes fall on the Trowe his eyeless face scrunched up in a snarl at me.

"Narsi—"

"My mistress is alone while you sleep, Archangel," cutting me off, he snarls. "You protect Shadow now."

With one last hiss, he twirls around and disappears into the forest. Afraid for Helena, I jump to my feet, swaying dangerously. The weight from my wings, a soothing comfort I've had for millennia, feels like a burden now. My skin is tight with an itch I cannot scratch, but still I push off from the rough bark and stumble after the spirit. The tips of my wings drag on the forest floor and each step is more painful than the last, but I continue forward with just one glance in Eric's direction. Still covered, with his skin matching the night, he blends in with the thick roots around him. Whatever made Helena cover us will not let anyone see him unless someone is right on top of him. I convince myself he will be fine and that Helena is more important.

Catching a glimpse of the Trowe in the distance, my labored breaths seesaw from my lungs. Fists clenched, fingers aching from the force, I hurry after him. The confusion I felt with my waking prevented me from paying attention to anything else apart from my immediate surroundings. Now, I cannot ignore the screams and shouts that raise the short hairs on my arms and neck. Because of my itching and burning skin, I know where we are. Just like

I knew where we'd end up before we even crossed the portal.

Hell.

Whatever I once thought I would feel when I entered hell is absent. I do not feel dread or fear in this realm. Nor do I feel disgust. The only thing I sense is my light shrinking, and that comes from the decisions I've made and my recent actions. My skin is also losing its luster, and the feathers on my wings are limp. I swallow down the unease, though. It doesn't matter. Nothing matters anymore but taking Helena where she belongs.

Another shriek pierces the air, its echo spreading like a mullet hitting a gong with a deep resounding sound the further it travels. My foot catches on a rock and pitches me forward, my shoulder slamming into the nearest tree. Hugging it like a long-lost brother, I pant, grinding my teeth when I straighten up. It's not really a good idea to stumble around making noise like I am, but with all the sounds coming from around me, I hope mine are just a note in a horrifying song of the night.

Bright light illuminates everything around me. The tall trees hide most of it when my head jerks up, but nothing can hide the forking veins spreading through the dark sky like a spiderweb. The harsh scent of ozone burns my nostrils and sends a hard punch to my chest. Pushing fatigue down, I jog in the direction it comes from while praying that she is not hurt. A humorless laugh is stuck in my throat at the thought of me praying right now. I am long past my time of redemption. Pretty sure I missed that about two portals ago.

I hear the thumping footsteps too late. One moment I'm tattering like a drunk human in my attempt to find Helena, and in the next two demons—one male and one female—

burst from the shrubbery where they come face to face with me. I'm unsure who is more shocked at the encounter, honestly. Seeing an angel on their path is definitely alarming for them, but I'm stunned for seeing demons here, too, especially when I don't think there will be anyone else occupying the realm. I gape at them in the same way they gape at me, at least until I notice the horrified look on the female's face. I cannot look that intimidating with limp wings and swaying feet, unless … maybe I look pathetic enough to make any female shrink in pity for me.

The male demon pushes the female behind him, his body coiling up to attack. My spine snaps to attention, hands crackling with power in an instant. I have no right to harm them in their own realm because it's me that shouldn't be here, but instinct takes over before I can stop it. Claws as sharp as any blade press on my jugular, heat warning me too late that there's a body behind me. Hot air seers the skin of my shoulder and warm wetness trickles down my neck when the talons slightly part my skin. The male demon in front of me relaxes his stance, the relief palpable on his rugged face.

"Go." Eric's deep voice almost makes me turn to look at him in shock. His claws holding my life in his hands keep me in place. "I've got this one. Go take your female to safety."

"Thank you, Shadow." The male demon bows, then drops on one knee, the female following suit. "You are back." Lifting his head and with horns curling at his temples, he stares at Eric with a reverence that almost buckles my knees. "We might just survive. I will spread the word."

My mouth opens to tell him not to say a word about any of us being here when another burst of light blinds me, bright spots dancing in front of my eyes for long moments. When I can finally see, the male and the female are gone and Eric's claws are no longer on my neck. With my right hand crackling, green tendrils snake weakly through my fingers. I brush them over my neck, rubbing the blood between them after the cut is healed.

"Where is she?" Eric asks from behind me.

"Thank you." Pivoting to face him, his eyes snap down to stare at me still rubbing my blood with three fingers. "I'm looking for her. I just woke up, too. She had us hidden under the tree with Narsi watching over us. I'm hoping she is not too far."

"I hope so too." He swallows thickly and I frown at the reaction.

"Demons will harm her? I thought your mark would chase them away." My heart punches my ribcage with the force of a battering ram.

His eyes lock on something over my shoulder and, with a stomach full of dread, I turn around slowly. The forest illuminates from an approaching light. As it sidesteps a wide, ancient tree, I zero in on Helena where she has her back pressed so hard to it I think she wants to disappear inside it. Her eyes are squeezed shut, too, making me suck in a sharp breath.

"Demons won't harm her," Eric growls menacingly. "But Angels will."

One of my brothers stops parallel to Helena, his head turning to face her. The victorious smile on his face holds no warmth. Numbness takes me. Eric launches from next to me, becoming a dark blur between us. The angel's sword lifts in the air, lightning spitting in short bursts from the tip. Helena's eyes snap open and lock on mine.

My heart stops at the sight.

Golden eyes, angel eyes, stare at me from her face.

Chapter Eighteen

ERIC

I barrel at the angel, somehow completely missing him. Instead, I hit the trunk of a tree with enough force that branches and leaves shower over my head. Jumping to my feet, I whirl around and stop dead in my tracks. My mate's eyes are glowing like two suns on her dirt-smudged face. The palm of her hand is pressed on the flat blade of the sword, holding it away from her, while her other hand is on the Angel's shoulder as she forces him down on one knee. I can see the strain on his face while he tries to shake her off him.

Helena's face looks serene, almost calm and comforting, which is a stark contrast to this place. The Angel releases his hold on the weapon and twists out of her grip. His wings snap open, a blur of golden glow and white fucking feathers, and I place all my weight on the balls of my feet ready to spring at him. Another pair of wings whirls in front of me, this one familiar, and I watch in amazement when Raphael and the Angel clash with a resounding boom. The power when they collide plasters my back on the trunk behind me, the rough bark scraping my back and wings.

"Stand down." Raphael unleashes the voice of an Archangel, the sound of many voices speaking as one washing a shiver down my spine.

Towering over the weaker angel, he glowers at him, his fingers tightening around the smaller male's neck. Raphael might've looked weak staggering through the forest, but I can't see any of it right now. Braced above the male, he is imposing enough that I'll even think twice about taking him on. Then something shifts next to him. My jaw drops when I see my mate with her hand pressed on Raphael's arm. A golden glow pulses from her and wraps around the Archangel, feeding his radiance while I watch.

"The portals have opened, Raphael," the angel snarls, and loathing twists his features. "This is our chance to be rid of the vermin once and for all." His gaze burning with hatred, he stares up at him. "Whose side are you on, bother?"

"Mine." Shock holds me mute when Helena smiles softly at the angel.

"You shouldn't even exist." The angel sneers, baring his teeth at her. "This is what has befallen the realms because of you, and now the righteous will win. Good *will* conquer."

Her head tilts curiously as she watches him for a long moment. I hold my breath, wanting nothing more than to go to her, but instinct holds me in place. Something is happening here that I don't understand and the last thing I want to do is hurt her by trying to protect her. She will laugh in my face for finally learning my lesson if she can hear my thoughts. Those golden eyes of hers flick in my direction, one side of her lips twitching like she has heard me. My eyebrows hit my hairline. What the actual fuck is going on?

"You know"—Turning her attention back to the angel, she muses conversationally—"a friend told me the same thing once. Not that long ago actually. That good will always win." Her lips purse in thought as she gives the angel a onceover. "I must say I agree."

Gut tightening painfully, my blood moves sluggishly through my veins at those simple words. Does she despise me now? Why is she glowing like an angel? We saved her from the djinn but who knows what those fuckers did to her. Did I find her just so I can lose her again? For good this time, since even Death couldn't keep us apart thanks to Raphael. Speaking of which.

The Archangel's wide eyes are staring at me in shock, and I admit it matches my own. That's when I realize it's not him strangling the life out of the smaller angel. My mate is controlling his body by a simple touch.

"Even she agrees, Raphael." The angel gasps, sipping air through his mostly closed throat. "Release me."

The ground under my feet shudders, the trees whispering when their crowns tremble from the quaking roots. The glow from the two angels and Helena seems to brighten as everything else around us darkens more. With a deep breath, I call the shadows to me, bracing for whatever is coming. To add to the weirdness of the night, some of them break away from me and swirl around her ankles like excited pets. Unable to help myself, I scratch at my horns. Nothing like this has ever happened before. Not even my father can command my shadows.

"I said the good will win." Shaking her head like the angel is a disobedient child, I see her fingers twitching like she is missing something in her hand. Her dagger, I realize when they brush near her thigh. "I never said *you* will win."

"I am made of Heaven." The angel's voice is raspier. "I am what good is made of."

"Ah, but you see, I have many friends. Another one told me that evil has many faces." The intensity in her gaze shrivels even my own lungs. "I tend to agree with them both. And you may be made of light, angel, but good you are not. Heaven's hands are washed in too much blood to be able to claim it just for themselves."

"Your soul will burn for eternity." Newfound strength comes to the angel, but his cursed words make me snarl. "You will never know peace if you raise your hand against Heaven."

"Nor will I know peace if I stand and watch." The glow around her sends a strong pulse through the darkness, and Raphael's hand jerks once, ripping the angel's throat.

Horror and acceptance war on his face as his front is bathed in blood. The angel drops in a heap on the forest floor, his eyes fading to dull sockets and staring sightlessly at my mate. Mouth open in a silent scream, he looks frozen in place as his skin shrivels, light bursting from it and hitting Raphael at the center of his chest. Helena holds her hand pressed on the Archangel until the energy disappears, then she crouches next to the husk at her feet, fingers trailing down the Archangel's body.

"You see, angel. There's something everyone has forgotten to tell you, and that is the devil is in the details. Thank you for giving your lifeforce to heal Raphael. He needed it." With those words, her eyes roll to the back of her head and she drops on the ground.

Raphael ends up on his ass next to her, eyes almost popping out of his head. Dropping on my knees I pull her into my lap, brushing lumps of hair away from her face. With lips slightly parted, her head rolls on my arm, arms hanging limply at her sides. I watch her, not even daring to blink until I see her chest rising in falling with her breaths.

"What the fuck was that, Raphael?" Grimacing, I don't dare look away from her.

"She controlled me." Bewildered, he barks out a mad laugh. "She controlled an Archangel with just a touch."

Dread eats me alive.

"My shadows went to her." Swallowing the lump in my throat, I cup her face. "They were dancing at her feet while she was touching you." The rough skin of my thumb catches on her skin. "She will be okay, right? I'll kill you myself if she's not."

"She will be okay, yes." Pushing off the ground, he lifts to his full height and looks down at me, flexing his arm as if testing them. "I'm not sure about you and I, but she'll be fine."

"What are you talking about?" Glaring at him, I see him pointing at something to the side.

"If one angel was running around here, there's bound to be more of them. I don't think hiding our presence is an option anymore."

"Fuck me!" spitting the words, I growl at the damn Haltija, who's grinning at me from afar. The idiotic thing grew in size again.

Chapter Nineteen

HELENA

Those two are hiding something.

Stomping with frustration, I glare at my feet, walking between Eric and Raphael. Monster boy moves in front of me as agile as a feline on the prowl. His large muscular arms swing gently with each shift of his wide shoulders, the clawed tips twitching restlessly. He also keeps giving me quick glances over his shoulder, probably trying to hide his worried gaze. Why he thinks this will work for him right now is beyond me. It certainly hasn't worked for him so far.

A soft snort escapes me, and I shake my head while still watching my feet. I can feel his burning stare on the top of my head, but I ignore him. Raphael clears his throat—because that's not obvious at all—and Eric continues his pace still staring at me.

The Archangel is stepping softly, his feet barely making a sound for someone his size. For the most part, he is lost in thought as we move through the forest, his face not giving anything away. It makes me wonder what happened, because I really can't remember. Besides the lightning, and I must've passed out from the bolt that zapped me, because one moment I was holding my breath, my fingers numbing from it, while in the next I was sprawled in Eric's lap, both of them looming over me with strange expressions. Oh, and my sidekick towering as tall as some of the trees, grinning as he glanced down at me. I have no idea what happened, but I'll wager a guess it has something to do with the blood covering Raphael like war paint.

"What's this place again?" Squinting at Eric's back like I have laser vision and I can see if he is lying, I twist the hem of the sack I'm wearing between my fingers. I feel restless so it gives my hands something to do.

"We are at the opposite side of the realm from Lucifer's home." Eric keeps his voice low, a soft hum coming off his chest and back with each word. "It's close to the pits of Hell, full of scum, rogues, and mercenaries."

"You mean opposite your *father's* home," I correct him, feeling Raphael's tension at Eric's explanation battering my back. "If I have to suck it up and accept calling Satanael my father, you will have to do it too." The conversation between the voices from before comes loud and clear in my head. "Speaking of which. Someone walked past me before you two found me. They were scared of Satanael as much as they were scared of the angels." I shiver at the thought, stumbling around when Narsi takes a step to follow us. One step every few minutes, lucky bugger. My feet are killing me.

Silence follows my words, alarms ringing like church bells in my head.

"Spill, Eric." To make sure he knows how serious I am, I shuffle faster and poke him between his ribs. "Start talking."

"After what happened …" his voice trails off, his hand rubbing at one of his horns in agitation. That was my cue that we are talking about the night I died. Well, when I ended up in Purgatory because I feel very much alive. Then and now.

"Okay." Prodding him to continue, I wait.

"Satanael and I might've given in to our instincts because of the grief." Cursing up a storm that almost makes me giggle like an idiot, he moves jerkily, all feline grace forgotten. "I stayed in the human realm where Raphael found me. Satanael came here looking for you."

"You seem sane to me," I point out. Maybe I should be worried more about the whole thing, but after everything, I'm emotionally drained. I have to be if I can't feel what I need to, even when I know it's important.

"I had an Archangel to bring me to my senses. He didn't," Eric throws the words over his shoulder dryly.

"No one could bring sense to the Archangel either," Raphael murmurs and I crane my neck to look at him. He gives me a tight smile. I don't buy it.

"Okay, so let's go find him and get his ass back on track." It makes perfect sense to me. "That's where we are going, right?" A jolt makes me jump when another scream echoes around us. I skip on the next step to cover it up, but the snort from behind me tells me I failed. I seriously don't know why I even try.

"No." Eric adds a chopping motion with his hand, as if the snappy word is not enough. "We are going to the portals on the other side and to the human realm. There is no need for you to be here longer than you have to."

"Why?" I laugh since obviously we are not trying for stealth. Narsi kind of kills that for us. "You scared my halo might get crooked if I stay here a bit longer?" My joke falls flat, ricocheting the tension by a hundred degrees. "Okay, you know what?" I sound shrill. "Enough with this bullshit. One of you better start talking or I'll scream until every soul in Hell comes to find us. This is fucking ridiculous. What the hell is going on?"

"You will do no such thing, Helena." Eric whirls on me, but what stuns me speechless is him saying my name in anger. "If demons come, I'm not sure I'll be able to protect you and Raphael as well on my own." My finger starts lifting so I can point at Narsi, but the reddening of his face makes me drop my hand. "If angels show up, he can't protect both of us either. It's not safe here."

Raphael sucks in a breath, I guess to argue the point as well, but Eric looks pointedly from the Archangel to me, deflating his sails. They glare at each other for a moment and I fold my arms over my chest. When they finally grace me with their attention, I lift an eyebrow, my foot tapping impatiently. Their scowls deepen.

I purse my lips.

"Infuriating female," Eric bursts out as he throws both arms in the air.

"Really?" My lips press in a firm line. "You can do better Eric, try it. Think of a better insult."

"It's not an insult." Grabbing me by the upper arms, he shakes me. The gentle way I move contradicts his furious face. "All the realms are just like this one. Every portal is open. You can find a fight there as easy as you'll find one here."

Fear flickers through his burning gaze, silencing my protest that it shouldn't matter where we are if everywhere is the same. I look from him to Raphael. Eric is as stubborn as I am, so there's no way I'll convince him to do anything unless he is willing to budge. The Archangel, however, is a different story.

"I need to know, Raphael." Pleading with him, I ignore the snarling Eric. Not long ago, I would've screamed in terror if I had a horned demon snapping at my face like a rabid dog. Now, I'm trying hard not to slap him. He is so lucky I can't stab him right now with something.

"You were not unconscious when we found you." Raphael sighs, rubbing a hand over his face as haggard lines form around his mouth.

"Raphael ..." Eric growls and I none to gently slap a hand over his mouth while I look at the Archangel expectantly.

"You controlled me with a touch to neutralize the threat," he says simply, watching me with no expression on his face. I blink at him. Then I blink again.

"You killed an angel while using Raphael to do it." Eric looks defeated when my eyes bulge out of my head. "He wanted to kill you," he adds, as if that makes things right.

"I'm not a djinn." I have no idea why I feel the need to point that out.

"We know you're not." When I don't comment, Raphael sighs again, his next words wrenched from his mouth. "It was an angelic power."

"You are one of the strongest Archangels, so what kind of an angelic power is that?" I ask him faintly.

"We can help you figure it out," a strange voice rasps from between the trees, and it's followed by a few humorless chuckles.

The three of us whirl around, Eric and Raphael stepping in front of me like idiots. I mean, they just told me I was able to control an Archangel. Doesn't that mean I should stand next to them at least, if not in front of them. I catch a glimpse of five demons in total, four male, one female, all dressed in leather and covered in weapons from head to toe. Eric can argue as much as he likes, but I'm not leaving this place until my father gets his head out of his ass. And these demons have what I need. Weapons.

"Oh, how nice of you to offer," I chirp from behind my two-asshole wall. "I personally would love your help."

Chapter Twenty

HELENA

"You assholes lied!" I call out to Eric and Raphael as I scramble up the tree, almost falling down and breaking my neck when the thin branch I'm using to haul myself up snaps under my weight.

I can feel the air stirring under my foot where the female demon tries to make a grab for it. Our assailants split up. Two of the males went after Eric, two after Raphael, leaving the female, who is roughly my height, to go after me. I stand there like an idiot waiting for my incredible power to go all badass and kick everyone's ass until she almost rips half of my face off with her claws. Leave it to Eric and Raphael to give me a bullshit story just so they don't have to tell me the truth.

Climbing from one branch to the next, I get as high up as I can so she won't be able to snatch my foot. Blowing a breath out, I peek through the leaves at the fight below while still keeping an eye on the demon circling my tree. Either none of them saw Narsi, or they are ignoring him.

It's not like you can miss the Trowe, so I'll go with the ignoring.

The demons fighting Eric glide around him, flipping daggers as long as my forearm from one hand to the other while they wait for an opening. He looks almost bored, barely moving, just enough to have them in his line of sight. The other two are not as patient. They jab their weapons at Raphael from both sides at once, but the Archangel dances away twice, almost causing them to impale themselves instead of him.

My head jerks down when the tree shakes, just in time to see the demon scrambling her way up the trunk the same way I did, curved dagger held between two rows of petite but sharp, pointed teeth. Her hair is shaved on the sides, left longer at the top between a set of short horns landing like a rat's tail on her back. Her red eyes glitter with the promise of violence when they focus on me. I wiggle my butt on the branch and pray it doesn't break as I wait. Her smile grows, probably because she thinks I've given up on my escape attempt. A husky chuckle comes from her when she gets close enough to believe that she has me cornered with nowhere to go.

I pick this branch because there are two others as thick as my arm jutting out from either side of it, and I am worried if Narsi moves that I'll fall down when the ground trembles. Now I'm glad for my smart thinking. Her foot pushes her up another foot and I take my chance. Grabbing hold of the two smaller branches, I put my weight on them, pull my foot back, and kick out with as much force as I can. My heel connects with her nose and jars my teeth, the crunching sound sending an adrenaline rush through me. With a muffled squeak, I plant my ass back down because I'm scared I'll drop down. The demon shrieks, blood gushing down her face and her eyes widening as she plummets to the forest floor.

I can't believe my luck when I catch a glimpse of the dagger balancing peculiarly on top of a bunch of leaves. As careful as I can, I slide down one branch, and then another so I'm level with it. My fingers cramp when I stretch my body to try to reach for it. It takes me two tries, but I finally snatch it by the blade, slicing the shit out of my thumb. Hooting excitedly, I scramble back to my safe spot.

"A ha!" Pushing thick leaves out of my face, I wiggle the weapon so Eric and Raphael can see it. "Look what I got!" Chuckling merrily, I wince as Eric almost gets stabbed when his head snaps in my direction.

Teeth bared, I give him a forced smile while mouthing sorry. Not that he sees it. His two demons redouble their efforts, jumping at him one after another. I narrow my eyes when I see Eric and Raphael murmuring something. Are they talking to the demons or between themselves? I glance quickly to make sure my red-eyed female is not climbing up again but she's sitting on the roots with two fingers pinching her bleeding nose while she glares at me. I guess she decided to wait me out. Good luck with that. My feet are killing me from all that walking, so I can sit here as happy as a clam for days.

A roar of pain brings my attention to the fighting again. I guess they were talking between each other. Until now, it appears they have only been toying with the demons. Both of them twirl around the assholes that think it's smart to attack us. The demons don't look as gloating as they did before, and the one on Raphael's side is even holding the left side of his ribcage with his arm wrapped around it.

"About time," I call out encouragingly. "Just knock them out already."

Eric and Raphael are like killing machines, one light and the other one dark. They pivot, twist, and turn, their bodies moving in ways that defy gravity, avoiding everything the demons throw at them. Sticking my bleeding thumb in my mouth, I gag when dirt and who knows what gets on my tongue. By the time I'm done cleaning it on my forearm, all four demons are dead. Monster boy and the Archangel don't even look winded. You'd never guess they were unconscious to the point I had to drag their heavy asses to hide them.

Just as the last demon hits the ground, they both turn all their focus on the female. The poor soul is still glaring at me with venom in her burning gaze. It's obvious she has no idea what is coming for her. Giving her a bright smile, I point so she can take a look. She glances really fast without paying much attention, then she does a double take. Her eyes snap to my face. My smile is so wide at this point that it hurts my cheeks.

When she tries to bolt from under my tree, Eric puts a burst to his step and with his wings he grabs her by the neck. His arm cocks back, claws gleaming and ready to strike. For the first time, I take a good look at the female demon.

"No, wait!" Eric's hand stops an inch from her throat, and I curse as I wiggle off the branch. "Don't kill her, wait."

Trusting he won't do it since he knows I have a dagger and he might expect me to stab him in the ass if he does, I carefully find my way down. Releasing the last one, I bounce on the ground to keep my balance and speed up, circling her. Raphael is watching me curiously while Eric widens his eyes and raises his eyebrow, looking more than impatient as he holds his claws at her throat.

"I need her clothes." The leather pants with straps for

weapons and the tight black sleeveless shirt will fit me perfect. "And her boots." I'm so tired of the shapeless sack that I'm already pulling it off me.

"I can kill her first." Eric growls in irritation, relaxing a bit when he sees Raphael give me his back the second the sack reaches my upper thighs.

"Eww, that'll be like grave robbery. No one wants to wear clothing from a corpse, monster boy."

"She'll die two seconds after it."

"But she is breathing now." I wave my hand for her to hurry.

She shoots daggers at me, not moving a finger. I turn to Eric expectantly and his eyebrows crawl up his forehead.

"Should I undress her?" He sounds so offended I almost laugh.

"You can go if you give me your clothes." Seeing she doesn't believe me, I offer her another solution. "I can ask Raphael to hold you by the neck if you'll trust that more."

I've never seen anyone strip so fast. As soon as I say the Archangel's name I blink. When I open my eyes, she is barefoot in her underwear.

"Let her go, Eric." Stabbing my legs in the pants, I wiggle them over my hips. "Spread the word wherever you go that Helena is looking for Satanael. Better yet, if you see him, make sure you point him in our direction." Pulling the shirt over my head, I have to shove my boobs up a bit because the fabric is a little tight across my chest. "Let her go, now."

Eric is not even paying attention. His eyes are still locked on my boobs, burning with hunger and sending frenzied butterflies flapping around in my lower belly. In hopes to hide my face from him, I turn my back and duck, bending down to pull on the boots. No more stepping on rocks.

"I can't believe I let her go. This is trouble waiting to happen," Eric says from right behind me just as I hear the demon run for her life.

"It's not like we never have trouble." Lacing the boots, I don't lift my head.

"Very true, cupcake." A loud slap bounces off the trees when his large hand connects with my ass and jerks me upright. Of course the stretched leather makes the slap sound a lot stronger than my tingling butt cheek feels.

Chapter Twenty-One

ERIC

Steering us clear of the sounds of the continuing battle, I lift my face up, nostrils flaring as I scent the air. The clawing stench of blood and decay drifts on the breeze that occasionally passes through the trees. Helena hasn't said a word since we left the idiot demons, and I'm still unsure why they thought it would be a good idea to take me and Raphael on. Don't mercs have more brains that that usually?

"Wouldn't it be better if the two of you fly?" Helena speaks suddenly, pulling me out of my thoughts.

"We should keep to the ground." Scanning our surroundings, I don't turn to her. It gets more difficult to suppress my need to hold her close. "Narsi is a beacon as it is, but he looks menacing enough to be left alone for now. I think the mercenaries believed he was stalking us as well, that's why they decided to attack first."

"We should not have left the female to run amok," Raphael muses from the back. "Speaking Helena's name through the realm might get Satanael's attention, but it'll bring Mammon on our trail."

"Oh, wouldn't that be wonderful." When I glance back, Helena twirls her new-found dagger with a big smile on her face. "He and I have a lot of unfinished business to discuss."

"We should find a place to rest if we are staying here to look for your father. You need to relax." Punctuating it with a pointed look at her, I rack my brain to try to think of a safe place to take her in this part of the realm. It's been a very long time since I have been here.

"I feel perfectly fine, Eric." She smirks at me. "Actually, I feel better than I've felt for years if I'm being honest. It's the two of you I'm worried about. A few hours ago, both of you were out cold. I was the one dragging your assess around. Also, you are both heavy as hell, just for the record. Especially you, monster boy."

"I'm still not sure why that happened." My attention zones in on the fidgeting Archangel who's avoiding my eyes. "Passing through a portal has never been that difficult, or that painful before. Now that I think about it, not even my first passage was that bad. Disorienting yes, but I've never had my insides shredded from it."

"You've never passed through the portals of Purgatory, either," Raphael says in a soft voice, and the words are so low I can barely make them out, even with the daring tilt of his chin. "It's different than the rest."

"Different how?" My mate has turned her focus on him now and he stills, washing all emotions from his face. The heat in the air spikes us slightly and she narrows her eyes on him. "Different how, Raphael?"

"Those portals are made to accept everything passing through, coming inside the realm." A muscle jumps in his jaw, and he stabs his fingers through his hair, making it stick out funnily on top of his head. "They're not meant to let anything go out."

Helena snorts, her amusement dying as fast as it started when the Archangel keeps his gaze steadily on her face. My gut plummets to my feet, but the fucker is pointedly ignoring my glare. I had a feeling he was up to something and this just drives that home. He better hope that this doesn't come and bite us in the ass. I'll rip his feathers out one by one if a hair goes missing from Helena's head. Realizing I'm rubbing at my chest, I let my hand drop to my side. Based on the stiffening of Raphael's shoulders, he doesn't miss the movement.

"Ever?" Helena's question caught me off guard.

"What?"

"The portal doesn't allow anyone out of the realm ever? Or has someone gone through it before?" She lifts her hand, one fingernail aimed toward her mouth as if she will start biting it, but she catches herself before she does. "Well?"

"Never." Raphael sighs a gust of breath that rushes out from him. "No one has left it before."

Helena walks calmly to the closest tree, lowering herself down with even, precise movements. All my instincts go on alert, the hairs on the back of my neck prickling like a silent predator has me in its sights. It's as unsettling as Raphael's words.

"No." I scan the area around us, my eyes probing the darkness as I search for the threat. The Archangel continues. "There is no one around, Eric." My head snaps in his direction. "I feel it as well, but I believe it has nothing to do with a silent threat. We are both feeling her displeasure."

"What are you talking about?" My chest vibrates because of the deep growl in my voice, but he only watches me with an unreadable face.

"I'm not sure." Raphael starts pacing, fists clenched at his sides. "I started feeling it from the moment I woke up here. I couldn't figure it out. Honestly, I thought it was because I was disoriented. But it gets stronger the longer I'm awake. Her urgency, fear, anger ... it effects my own emotions. That's why I've been observing her silently."

"Oh good," Helena chirps dryly. "Then you can both feel how badly I want to beat you across the head with one of those sticks right now." Her finger stabs the air as she points at a thick branch not far from her.

"I regret nothing."

Raphael clenches his jaw while staring her down, and I move swiftly to kick the broken part of the tree further away so she can't reach it. She rolls her eyes at me but says nothing, although she keeps her scowl on the Archangel. Better him than me, I suppose. I'll have my own problems to worry about when she hears about what happened while she was gone. No doubt the too-good fucker will inform her of it. If not him, I bet Beelzebub can hardly wait to see her.

"Who is ruling Purgatory?" Wrapping her arms around her curled-up knees, Helena turns from Raphael to me and back. "It looked to me like the djinn were going in and out of it just fine."

"They were coming in, yes. We saw none of them leaving it," Raphael says what I am thinking.

"But we left." The breath clogs my throat when her familiar green eyes swirl with gold, casting a faint glow on Raphael's face. "You knew that you could leave the realm when you decided to come looking for me. Right, Raphael?"

Only the rising and falling of the Archangel's chest is the answer. They stare at each other for a long time, none of them breaking eye contact. My head is spinning, every muscle in my body coiling up and hardening the longer the silence continues.

"Right? You knew that even if you couldn't find me, you'd be able to leave." She straightens her back as she speaks, my skin burning as if acid is being sprayed on it. I can feel my upper lip curling over my teeth. "Because you didn't just come alone, you also brought Eric with you."

"I regret nothing." His wings open and close jerkily, his power bouncing off him like a heartbeat while he looks down his nose at her.

"Answer my question damn you!" My heart skips a beat at her scream.

"No!" Roaring, Raphael throws his hands in the air angrily. "I didn't know that I would find you. And yes, I knew I would not be leaving the realm. It was a risk I took willingly. Your mate was lost to his grief, so it was a mercy to take him with me." The accusing finger at my face makes me snarl at him. I'm going to kill the fucker.

Helena is frozen, her mouth open in horror. Raphael whirls, slamming his fist into the nearest tree, the wide trunk splitting down the middle from the impact and making leaves and twigs rain down on him. All the fight drains from him, his shoulders hunching when he leans on the tree, head hanging low on his chest.

"I was willing to never leave Purgatory." The Archangel's voice is broken. "If I found you, I was going to do everything to get you out, but I accepted my fate to stay there. A life for a life. One soul for the other. That was my sacrifice." Blowing out a harsh breath, he barks out a humorless laugh. "And now here I am. I do not know what all this means. Why, after all my failures, I would be given another chance. I would be lying if I said I wasn't happy to be here, but I question it. What else is left for me to suffer to atone for my sins? How much is left of my pure soul to be tainted with my shortcomings?"

"You thought my life was worth more than yours? More than Eric's?" Helena's whispered words slice through me, the unshed tears evident in her voice.

"You are the balance, Helena." His face turns so he can look at her, cheeks sunken and gaze empty. A hole opens in my chest. "Whatever Zedkiel and Satanael were hoping to achieve, I do not think they accounted for what would happen if you survived long enough to make your mark on the realms. None of us did. I did it for all of us. But I am selfish because I mostly did it because of myself ... for the promise I made ... for the love I still have for your mother."

"Thank you." They both look at me when I speak, the words wrenched out of the center of my being. "Whatever your reasons, Archangel, thank you for bringing my mate back to me."

Raphael searches my face for long moments before giving me a jerky nod. Pushing off the tree, he straightens and rubs his hands over his head, shaking off the leaves stuck to it. Helena sits still, her unseeing eyes staring off into the distance. With one more glance, the Archangel turns his back on us and strides away.

"I'll be back. I need a few moments alone."

Chapter Twenty-Two

HELENA

I watch Raphael disappear, the darkness of the forest swallowing his body. I'm not even sure how I'm supposed to feel right now. Each word he says is initially like a slap in my face, bubbling anger in my chest until I feel like I'm going to explode from it. But the longer I sit here staring at nothing, the more lost I am. What in the hell possesses him to think anyone's life is worth more than his?

"That's so much like Raphael, huh?" When I turn to Eric, his form shimmers, the human form replacing all the wings, claws, and horns as he comes to sit next to me.

"What is?" Reluctantly, he lifts his arm and waits for me to accept his touch or not.

A lump forms in my throat.

I've been so self-centered, consumed by all the fear, anger, and everything else coming my way that I didn't even stop to think how all this feels to him. To Raphael. Or anyone else in general. What my death may mean to any of them. With a sigh, I wiggle closer and tuck myself under his arm, pressing my face in the hollow of his neck. Warmth washes over me when his scent fills my lungs, his fingers giving my arm a reassuring squeeze. He is still stiff as a board, like he expects me to bolt at any moment. I feel like shit.

"To put everyone else before himself." Murmuring the answer to his question, my lips grazes his skin and he shivers. "I'm sorry, Eric."

"For what?" Pressing his chin down, he tries to look at me but I shove my face closer to his skin.

"For being a shitty person with an attitude. The two of you came to a realm with no way out looking for me and all I've done is talked shit. So, I'm sorry."

"As long as my eyes can see you, and as long as you are in my arms, you can do whatever you want, Hel." His arm tightens around me. "You are handling this much better than any of us would've."

"What does that say about me?"

"That you are much tougher than you give yourself credit for, to start with." Relaxing slowly, he gets more comfortable by pulling me over his chest. "None of this has been easy on anyone, least of all you. You sacrificed your life to protect us all. No matter what Raphael says, whatever fates are weaving the thread must admire that about you."

Snorting ungracefully, I burrow closer to his warmth. The man is like a furnace, and when my cold nose presses against his skin, he flinches.

"I'm not what you make me out to be, Eric." Tracing my fingers over his abs, I watch his muscles jump and twitch. "The more I think about it, the more the line blurs between what I've done and what the djinn are doing." When he stiffens, I press my palm on his stomach. "I haven't done anything for the sake of hurting someone on purpose, but how is it any different? I have fought and killed just to get the world to be like I want it to be. Who's to say my way is the right way? Who am I to decide what's right and what's wrong? I'm doing the same thing they are, trying to make it the way they think it should be."

"There is nothing similar between you and that scum," he spits angrily. "There is not a mean bone in your body, Hel. Everything you've done shames me for the reckless centuries I've spent roaming the Earth. You've shown mercy when there was no hope for it. Even Heaven should feel humbled by that."

"Mercy is for the weak. Look where it got us." His weight presses on my chest making it difficult to breathe.

"The weak have no room for mercy. It takes more strength to lower your weapon than to take a life. I am weak. You, my mate, are stronger than all of us combined."

"I thought you went ape shit after I was gone." Trying to lighten the mood, I poke him gently in the ribs. "Didn't know you studied philosophy and became a wise man."

Yelping from my probing fingers, he wiggles away, snatching my hand to stop me. His thumb rubs the top of my hand gently before pressing it on his stomach and covering it with his much larger one. I can feel the steady beat of his heart under my cheek.

"I had to up my game so you didn't ditch me for some glowing-feathered fuck." Voice laced with laughter, he kisses the top of my head. "All joking aside, Hel, from the moment I saw you, you've made me want to be a better male. Not to prove anything to anyone, but to be good for you. Nothing in all my centuries has made me want to change my ways."

Lifting my head, I look up at him, his deep green eyes so much like the leaves in the forest around us as he searches my face. My chest feels tight from his softly spoken words and all the emotions I see swimming in those depths. He has done more than I thought possible for me. Stood by me when even my own kind has turned their back. Held my hand when the ground under my feet disappeared. And he hasn't let go once. Not even now, when we have no idea what all of this means. Heartbeat steady, he stands next to me, a sturdy presence. A pillar I can lean on to keep me safe when the storms hit from all sides.

His face blurs from the tears swimming in my eyes before they spill over and trickle down my cheeks, wetting his skin. Lifting his hand, he cups my face with his hand while his thumb wipes them away. He doesn't say a word, but he doesn't need to. Come hail or high tides, he will continue to be that pillar for me without judgment, without doubt.

"I love you." At my words, he closes his eyes and takes a deep, shuddering breath. My heart breaks at the relieved expression on his face.

"I love you more than life itself, Hel. I cannot live without you." His green gaze bores into mine, the intensity taking my breath away.

The knot inside me unravels, the uncomfortable feeling that I carried with me from the moment I blinked my eyes open in that tunnel disappearing. It's easier to take a breath, my skin fitting comfortably over my bones instead of being stretched too tight. No matter what happens, as long as he is by my side we will figure out things together. Forgetting all about the battles raging in this realm, about Raphael or Narsi, I pull my hand from under his.

"Make love to me, Eric." I twist around and crawl over his lap. "I need you."

Chapter Twenty-Three

HELENA

Eric studies my face so long I start fidgeting on his lap. When he says nothing, I turn to get off him, but his hands snatch my arms lightning fast and hold me in place. I lift my head to look at him and my stomach flipflops at the intensity of his gaze. It sends a shiver rushing up and down my spine and raises goosebumps on my arms and legs. Heat gathers between my thighs that are pressed on him.

The hunger in those green depths triggers my own, and a golden glow bathes his face. It's as sudden as the slight widening of his eyes, but he doesn't give me time to ponder on it. He crashes his lips on mine, thick fingers spearing in the hair on the back of my head. Grabbing a fistful, he angles my face to his liking and I part my lips to welcome him. His tongue glides and tangles with mine, the taste of him exploding in my mouth.

A deep appreciative groan vibrates from his chest to mine when I plaster myself to him, hungry for more. My hands are everywhere. I claw at his shoulders, his hot skin warming my hands. The fabric of my borrowed shirt feels tight, my pebbled nipples rubbing on it in exquisite pleasure pain, short-circuiting my brain. Surrounded by his scent and body, I lose myself to the need that is choking me.

His movements turn more urgent, the gentle way he is savoring the kiss getting rougher. Sucking on my tongue, he tilts his pelvis and, in one smooth move, flips me around using one of his hands to cushion the back of my head. Eric's weight settles deliciously on top of me, pressing me hard on the forest floor. Rocks and roots dig in my back, but his thick erection slides between my thighs in just the right place to erase any chance of discomfort. My core pulses, clutching at the emptiness I need him to fill.

He kisses my breath away, the glide of his tongue and press of his lips searing my soul. We have kissed many times, but never like this. Never like it's the last time our lips will touch, and never as if we don't want it to ever end. My nails press harder on the expanse of his back, the skin splitting under the sharp edges. He growls in my mouth, hips rolling and driving me further into the insanity that is overtaking all rational thought.

With more force than necessary, I rake my fingers down his back to his narrow waist. Abandoning my mouth, he presses openmouthed kisses down my neck to my shoulder where his teeth take hold of my skin. The pressure of his bite combines with the consistent movements of his hips, making me open my mouth in a silent scream even as a low, deep moan rips from my chest. Wetness drenches my core, my thighs getting slick in the leather pants.

"Eric …" Gasping his name, I have no idea what I'm asking him to do. Keep doing what he is doing or more.

His hand disappears from the back of my head, sliding over my shoulder and down my side to push my shirt over my aching breasts before continuing down and grabbing my ass. He yanks me harshly to him, his erection hitting hard on my clit. This time a real scream bursts from my lips. My hands fumble with his pants, tugging frantically at the damn button and zipper. The moment they give way, my fingers slide inside and wrap around his cock that jumps at the touch pulsing in my palm.

With a snarl, Eric yanks on my pants, the buttons easily popping open as he pulls them down my legs. His lips don't leave my skin, kissing down my chest until his tongue swirls around the areola and he sucks the stiff peak in his hot mouth. Panting, I keep gliding my hand over his shaft, my legs jerking and kicking the pants off. The boots prevent me for taking them off, but I wiggle enough to loop my legs over Eric's. Having him skin on skin is not enough. I need more. I need all of him.

Guiding his cock to my entrance, I tilt my hips and he lifts his face up, pinning me with a half-lidded gaze. His lips are swollen from our kisses, the upper one lifted over his teeth in a snarl. The look on his face is so feral it sends a jolt of adrenaline through me, but he stands poised over me and doesn't move. Need is digging a hole in my chest and my core pulses, my insides burning from it.

"Never again ask me to give you up, Helena." His voice is as deep and as guttural as when he is in his demonic form.

My eyes widen at the sound.

"I will never let you leave me again. Not if Death himself is trying to take you away. Do you understand?" Shadows dance and pulse around him, a sight I've never seen unless his wings are out of his back.

"Eric …" I sound breathless and pathetic, but he doesn't budge, his cock hot and silky like velvet wrapped over steel.

132

In my hand, it jerks impatiently. I can't help but feel the same way.

"Never again, Helena," he whispers, not moving an inch.

Stubbornness at his manipulation rears its head and I move my hips up, trying to get him where I need him. He lifts slightly, just out of my reach. I choke on the frustrated scream that tries to push its way out, but he stares at me with all the patience of a saint. I never think he will do this, try to get his way while having me at his mercy, and I can only imagine how far I have pushed him for him to do it now.

"Never," he repeats, and the fear I see on his face breaks my heart.

"Never again, Eric." Tears swim in my eyes when he releases a shuddering breath. "I promise," I choke out.

"I'll never lose you again." His voice breaks, but I forget everything I am going to say when with one hard push, his cock fills me until our pelvic bones smash together, stretching me with as much pleasure as I can hope for to accommodate his girth.

Chapter Twenty-Four

ERIC

I lock my elbows and my knees so she doesn't feel the tremor that shakes me to my core. Everything reaches a crescendo inside me when I see her soft and naked under me, so strong yet still very much breakable. Too many times she has slipped through my fingers when I wanted nothing more than to keep holding onto her. And I do the one thing I promise myself I'll never do. I use my body and her need of me to manipulate her enough to give me a promise. My mate and the Archangel have one thing in common. They'll never go back on their word.

A deep groan comes from me when her heat wraps around my cock, her channel sucking me in like she never wants me to leave. This is where I want to be and where I plan to stay. She just doesn't know it yet. I have my doubts that I am good enough for someone like her. In those moments of weakness, I even try to push her away. What an idiotic thing to do. I may think I don't deserve her, but I'll be damned if I don't take what the fates have offered with both hands and rip the worlds apart in order to keep her. I understand what Raphael says all too well. At this very moment, all the anger I have towards him dissolves into nothing because I know I would've done the same. Nothing would have stopped me from going through that portal, not even if I knew life itself might vanish from existence.

With a snarl, I take Helena's mouth in a punishing kiss, my hips pumping roughly between her legs. Her small hands clutch at my back, nails running trails on my skin. It only drives me wilder. She gushes wetness, coating my thighs and sleeking her entrance more. Her back arches off the forest floor, lifting me up as well. Snaking my arm around her waist, I use her weight to speed up my movements, sinking deeper into her body. Her breasts are cushioning me to her soft and pliant body resting under my hard chest. The pebbled peaks poking my skin seek attention. Her moans and breathless whimpering fill my ears and I can't stop the satisfied sound rumbling inside me from spilling out.

Sliding my knees further apart, I push her thighs open wider, pistoning in and out of her like it's the last thing I'll do before I perish. Each slide of her tongue around mine and each breath we share only fuel me more. I want to consume her so we are never apart. I feel her body stiffen under me, her breath catching. She is so close to falling apart in my hands. I redouble my efforts, not giving her time to stop it from happening. I know she wants to prolong it, but she is crazy if she thinks I'll be done with her that fast.

Wrenching her face away from mine, her lips part and she squeezes her eyes shut tight as she screams my name. Her channel clamps around me hard, sucking me in and holding me there while it pulses until her body jerks in my arms. It's hard to pull out and push in again but I keep at it until she goes limp under me. The hold of her arms around me goes slack, fingers trailing gently over my back. With great effort and a strength I didn't know I possess, I pull out of her, my cock slapping my stomach in anger. Her eyes open slowly and she blinks at me with a soft smile on her face, one I plan to keep there.

Confusion forms a line between her eyebrows when I lift off her. Her half-lidded gaze slips from my face to my jutting erection sticking out of my body. Her lips part, no doubt to question my intention, but I don't give her time to speak. With one swift movement, I lift her off the ground, flipping her around and pressing her to the tree.

Then I'm inside her again, tilting her pelvis back with both hands before she can even turn to see me over her shoulder. Her mouth opens with a startled gasp before a low moan escapes her throat, making my sack tingle with need.

"Hold on to the tree or it'll shred your skin." I can barely talk from the clenching of my jaw.

Without questioning me, her hands press on the bark and she pushes back at me, giving as good as she gets. Keeping her pinned with one hand, I glide the other up her arched back to her shoulder where I take a better hold of her body. My movements are even and hard, and I can see her round breasts swaying with each slap of skin on skin. The sounds she makes only spur me on, but I force myself to take my time. I gave her hard and fast, so now I'm going to take my time.

I don't stop my pumping when I feel the Archangel getting near. The stiffness of my shoulders relaxes when I sense him drifting away again. Helena will have my head if she knows he almost found us naked, me balls deep inside her. I have no issues with that. Let him watch if he wants. Let him see who she belongs to. Possessiveness steals the breath from my lungs and I fasten my hips. The tingles start at the base of my spine, my sack tightening where it slaps against her. Gliding my fingers over her soft belly, I plunge them between her legs, soaking them in her wetness. I circle her engorged clit, pinching it gently with every second twirl on it. She sucks in a sharp breath and widens her stance, her pelvis tipping higher to get me deeper inside her. I can feel myself twitching inside her like a ticking bomb about to explode.

My fingers press harder between her outer lips, my movements faster and less coordinated. My hips pump harder, the slapping growing in volume while I hold my breath. I feel myself getting impossibly harder inside her and she stiffens. Her scream bursts my eardrums, my roar of her name silencing any sound in the realm. I clutch her to me, pulsing inside her for long moments before curling over her and pressing my forehead between her sweat-coated shoulder blades.

"I love you." Still hard as a rock inside her, I pepper her back with kisses while I hold her close. Even still, I can't stop myself from grinning like a fool when she whispers drowsily back.

"I love you, too."

Chapter Twenty-Five

HELENA

"Why are we going back, again?" Eric pipes in from my side, unable to hide the bounce in his step.

I shake my head every time he and Raphael lock gazes and Eric grins triumphantly at the Archangel, making my face burns hot enough it'll put the fires of Hell to shame. No way Raphael didn't hear my screams and begging for Eric to fuck me harder or faster. Not that I can remember exactly what I was saying. He has an uncanny way of switching my brain off, and the only thing I know when that happens is that I can't get enough of him. First Lucifer, Beelzebub, and Colt were unwilling witnesses of all the noise we make, then it was an entire safe house full of hunters, Fallen, and angels, and now it's Raphael.

"I need to talk to Narsi," mumbling, I find my borrowed boots fascinating, flinching when I hear Eric chuckle like an arrogant jerk while Raphael only sighs. "You are not being funny anymore. It's quite annoying actually."

"I said nothing." He doesn't even try to hide his grin

when I glare at him. My fingers tap on the hilt of the dagger and he smoothly takes a step out of reach.

Raphael chokes.

My head snaps in his direction and I frown when I realize he is not actually choking. He is trying to cover a laugh. This time, even the tips of my ears feel like they are burning and I duck my head down, letting my unbrushed hair hide my embarrassment. A roar of suppressed laughter bursts from Raphael and I whirl on him with my mouth hanging open. Eric joins him, both assholes chortling in my face. I'm seriously considering stabbing one or both of them in the ass right now.

"You are both jerks in case you didn't know." I sound shrill. "I can't believe this is happening. And you … you are an Archangel for Pete's sake," stuttering, I storm away from them cursing under my breath.

"It is okay, Helena." Raphael coughs in his attempt to stop laughing in my face. "I should've thought better of it and left the two of you alone sooner. You needed time together, and there is no shame in that. Love is nothing to be ashamed of."

I give him a pointed look over my shoulder, almost face-planting when the toes of my boots hit a large rock. Where the hell did Narsi go? He is huge, so there is no way we can miss him. The stupid Trowe disappeared while me and Eric had our moment of naked gymnastics. I can't blame Narsi but this is getting ridiculous.

The smile slips from Raphael's face and I feel a ping in my chest. I really should keep my big mouth shut. With a very serious look on his face, he clears his throat.

"I don't want to hear it," I snap at him.

He opens and closes his mouth a few times before

frowning at me. "There are things you do and those you do not. Love or no love."

"Right. Keep telling yourself whatever you want so you can keep drowning in your guilt and misery. Spare me the bullshit, you hypocrite."

If I wasn't so upset with him, I would've laughed at the shocked expression on his face.

"And, Helena is back," Eric chirps, making me wonder how his face doesn't hurt from his mouth being stretched in such a wide grin.

"I wish Maddison was here. She would've put both of you in your place with just a look. I'll have to ask her for tips next time I see her." Craning my neck, I try to see if I can spot Narsi through the thick trees.

"I'd say it's lucky her and Leviathan are gone from the human realm for the time being." The serious tone in Eric's voice turns my head his way.

"Why? So you can do stupid stuff?" He flinches at my raised eyebrow, the remaining humor disappearing completely.

"I ripped apart everything that was in my way after you were gone." Staring straight ahead his fluid movements turn wooden and choppy. "I would've done worse if Raphael didn't find me."

Watching where I'm going, I consider his words. I never delude myself with the idea that Eric is an angel. Well not a literal angel, but some saint that makes it his life mission to do good and save lost souls. He is Lucifer's son for God's sake, and a Prince of Hell. His moral compass may be screwed by his nature but, it has never been evil, or menacing for the sake of creating chaos or causing pain. I'm not sure I would have turned out the same if our roles were reversed.

My heart jackknifes in my chest with the realization that yes, I would've. Knowing myself, I would've maybe done worse even.

I let that thought swirl in my head while staying quiet. Both men move silently behind me, neither saying a word which gives me plenty of time to think.

"I have a feeling that being able to leave Purgatory is like a second chance for all three of us." I can feel the arguments burning on the tip of their tongues, but I plow on without giving them the time to voice them. "Why else would we be the only ones to get out without having to pay anything for it?" An uncomfortable burning feeling stabs between my shoulder blades, so I roll them to work my muscles and get rid of the stiffness.

"I cannot be sure that we will not pay for it," Raphael says softly, breaking the tense silence that follows my words.

"Well, whatever comes we will deal with it then. I can't worry about what-ifs right now." My feet slow down, my fingers wrapping around the hilt of the dagger strapped to my thigh. "We are about to have company."

"I don't hear anything," Raphael murmurs, sliding closer to me.

"Neither do I." Eric is right beside me in an instant, his face lifting and nostrils flaring. "I can smell them though." The snapping of wings being open tells me they are both trying to look as intimidating as they can. I still don't understand why my back tingles and tightens at the sound of their wings.

"Let's take cover so we know what we are dealing with." Raphael grabs my elbow and tries to steer me away from the wide path between the trees.

I jerk away from his grasp. "No." I have no idea why,

but I feel it in my bones that I should stay exactly where I am. "Stay here."

"Hel," Eric has time to only say my name before a whirl of movement bursts from the shrubbery zipping right for me.

Raphael shouts in alarm a moment too late to warn me to get out of the way before something hits me in the knees and I end up on my ass with a loud *oomph*. Biting my tongue, my mouth fills with blood while my teeth rattle in my head from the impact. When the dark spots disappear and allow my vision to clear, Narsi's face looms over me, his yellowed teeth on full display due to his huge smile.

"I's goosing to kills yous." My words are slurred from the thickness of my tongue.

"I found him for you, Mistress." He hisses happily, his creepy voice sending shivers through me.

"Found who?" Spitting the words, Eric lifts him up by the scruff of his neck, and Narsi's tiny legs kick angrily in the air.

"Satanael." Snarling at Eric, the Trowe keeps wiggling like a worm pulled out of the soil. "Put me down, Shadow. I'll eat your face."

"Nobody is eating anybody here." Jumping off the ground with both arms in the air, I pry my sidekick out of Eric's claws. "Calm down, Narsi. Where is Satanael?"

The Trowe wraps around me, his legs circling my waist and arms while tightening around my neck like a koala. His mouth opens but the voice coming out does not belong to him.

"Here I am." A voice out of my nightmares comes from behind the tall bushes on our right.

Chapter Twenty-Six

HELENA

I remember being terrified when I had to meet my father for the first time. The idea of seeing the Devil himself face to face makes me think of nothing else but red pitchforks and horns aimed at me to claim my soul. Not even fighting the hellhounds scared me as much as seeing Satanael. But I remember his face looking very much human with tousled blond hair and eyes the same color as mine.

That's not what steps out of the shrubbery, curdling my blood and rendering me mute in horror. Having doubled in size, the creature facing me has a very angelic face. But that's where the pretty ends. Horns like a ram's twist around his head and over his ears, ending with sharp points at the back of his head like a crown made of bone. The pointed tips of his ears poke from his blond locks and drape around his face in an almost feminine curl. Bunched-up shoulders as wide as a house are curved aggressively inward, while biceps the size of tree trunks—muscles twitching and all—are held to the side of a broad chest. Too many rows of abs lead to a narrow, tapered waist where something like a loin cloth wraps around toga style over thighs that can crush a skull. Instead of regular feet, bird-like ones with two toes at the front and one long one at the back—for balance is my guess—curl and uncurl in the packed dirt. Leathery wings with three tipped claws at the high points stretch behind him to make him look exactly like a bat out of Hell … if there are any bats in Hell with angelic faces and skin as red as freshly spilled blood.

I can see now where the stories about the Devil and his looks come from.

"Djinn," Satanael snarls at me, lips curling over fangs as long as my forefingers.

"Whoa, hang on just a second." Backpeddling, I find my voice really fast. "I'm not a djinn. Are you fucking insane?"

"I think Satanael has lost his marbles, Mistress," Narsi hisses conversationally. His ability to use human terminology in that creepy voice of his boggles my mind.

"No shit." I take another step back, and my father tracks my move with eyes burning as if he has two flames sitting right above his sharp cheekbones.

"Snap out of it Satanael, because otherwise you'll have to go through me to hurt her and I'm sure you don't want to do that." Raphael steps between us, allowing me to take a breath. My heart gallops against my chest.

Why is my back burning like this right now? Like I don't have enough shit to deal with.

"How very noble of you, angel." My body vibrates from how deep his voice is, the bass rocking me on my heels. "You can die first, just like my daughter died for your lies and ideals."

"I am not dead, you idiot." My shout is ignored, so I glance at Eric standing too still for my liking. He does that right before he goes nuts and rips everything apart.

My stomach does a freestyle flipflop at the thought. The last thing we need is to start killing each other. We have enough jerks trying to do it already, and they certainly don't need our help.

"Can you not tell the difference between your own blood and a djinn?" Raphael taunts him, starting to circle him with his weight balancing on the balls of his feet. "The mighty Satanael maybe isn't so mighty after all."

"Did he lose his mind," whisper-yelling at Eric, I inch closer to him. "Stop him before they kill each other."

"The time for talk is past." Satanael's lips curl up at the corners and the sharp tips of his fangs poke out.

Something moves behind him, disturbing the shrubs around his feet. I zero in on it. At first, I have no idea what I'm looking at, but I am wondering if something is trying to attack him from behind. Maybe it's a snake, but I will cheer it on if it stops the fight that is about to happen. Then it moves again. A tail. A freaking tail with a triangular tip twitches lazily behind Satanael like a cat on a Sunday morning. My brain goes numb. After everything, it's the tail that shocks me the most.

Raphael and Satanael collide in a blur of fists, feathers, and leathery wings. The creature that is my father takes hold of the Archangel's neck, his thick fingers, tipped with razor claws, digging in his skin. Raphael pulls his right arm back, golden and green energy coiling around his fingers and forearm like flames dancing over it. Uncaring about the blood trickling from his throat, his fist hits Satanael at the center of his chest and lifts him off the ground, flinging him back through the shrubbery until he hits a tree and drops on all fours. My father shakes his low-hanging head, making his hair fall over his shoulders and hide his face.

Eric pounces, sailing through the air with his body

arched back and his arms lifted over his head. His wings stream behind him like a cloak, snapping open at the last minute and giving him a strong push just as he slams both fists like a hammer on Satanael's back. Power blasts from them and hits me so unexpectedly that I end up on my back. Narsi scrambles to get off me, and I cry out when his bony knees shove into my stomach.

Sounds of flesh hitting flesh along with grunts and growls make me jump on my feet. I expect Satanael to be out for the count, but I am wrong. As soon as I blink, he is on his feet, fighting Raphael and Eric like a Tasmanian devil. It's a whirl of fists, claws, wings, and a tail. His freaking tail is lashing out and splitting Eric's chest in a long welt that's oozing blood as I watch. It doesn't stop my mate, but it does take my breath away.

More power dances on both of Raphael's forearms, the dancing coils larger than before almost reaching his shoulders. The Archangel steps in between Satanael and Eric just as my father is reaching for Eric's throat. Satanael's head rears back, an earsplitting roar rocking the ground under my feet. Slapping my hands over my ears, I watch the Archangel. Instead of hitting him, he simply shoves both palms on my father's chest. Another roar echoes, bouncing off the trees around us as Eric's shadows wrap around Satanael and restrain him as if they are metal bands tying his arms to his upper body. All three of them are breathing hard, their chests heaving, although Satanael is the only one who keeps snarling like a rabid beast.

Eric moves closer to my father and my mouth drops open. Narsi is standing to the side, his skinny body flinging wildly with each flick of Satanael's tail, his teeth clamped on it. My sidekick's bony fingers hold the appendage for dear life, and his scrunched-up face tells me it isn't easy for him.

Still, he doesn't let go even with my father doing everything he can to shake him off. Hysterical laughter bursts out of me as tears stream down my face.

All sounds stop, including the flipping movement of my father's tail as I laugh like I haven't laughed in years. My throat hurts and a stitch develops on my side from it. When I have no more strength to make a sound, I wipe my eyes only to see everyone staring at me like I've grown another head.

"What?" Gasping for air, I run my fingers under my eyes to get rid of more tears.

"Helena?" Satanael's rasp sounds disbelieving, part fear and part hope making all my humor disappear.

"We tried to tell you." Raphael points out in frustration while rubbing his neck and grimacing when he looks at his blood-coated fingers. "As always, everything has to be fists first with you. Only then will you take a second to think."

"Release me." He strains against Eric's shadows, muscles bulging from the effort.

Eric and Raphael look at him warily, and I can see them debating if it is smart while my father still twitches with violence. He hasn't taken his eyes off me and I stare at him for a long moment. The longer we wait, the more frantic his movements and the fear twisting his face breaks my heart.

"Let him go, Eric." I push myself up, swiping at my knees to clean the leaves and dirt stuck to the leather.

"Hel …"

"Let him go." The shadows disappear just as I take one step towards them.

I'm lifted in the air, surrounded with leathery wings and red skin as thick arms squeeze the air from my lungs. My embarrassing squeak is luckily drowned by Satanael's deep voice.

"It is you." He chokes out. "You are alive." His body trembles and my throat feels tight.

"I did tell you that. But do you listen? No. As usual." I pretend that I don't sound as choked up as him. Apart from Eric and Raphael a few times, no one has ever held me like they have the most precious thing in the world in their arms.

Like Satanael is doing now, clutching me like I'll disappear at any moment.

My mouth opens to say something, but I have no idea what because a furious shriek curdles the blood in my veins, making me stiffen in my father's embrace. Craning my neck, I see all three of them staring in the same direction, their faces twisted in rage, their jaws clenched, and their teeth grinding. Well, all of them except Narsi. He is still biting Satanael's tail.

"Mammon," Eric snarls.

"Let's not keep him waiting long." Raphael rolls his shoulders and cracks his neck.

"You need to let me go, big guy." Not knowing what to do, I slap Satanael's chest half-heartedly.

The smile he gives me leaves me debating if I should offer one back or scream in terror.

Oh Mammon, I would hate to be you right about now, I think to myself.

Chapter Twenty-Seven

HELENA

"You are breathing down my neck." Shoving Satanael back, I blow a frustrated breath out.

We came through the woods, nearing a place that the three jerks think we can find Mammon. And the whole time my father has been right on my heels, his arms at my sides like he's hovering in case, I don't know, I trip or something. Since he is still in his demonic form—he must calm his wrath in order to change forms, and those are his words not mine—it's freaky as fuck. I say three jerks because Raphael and Eric are enjoying this way too much. Walking just a step behind so they can watch the show better, they keep snorting, coughing, and chuckling.

I'm going to punch them in their teeth soon.

"Shhh ..." Raphael rushes in front of us and disappears through the foliage.

Ducking, all of us take cover, me holding my breath so I don't make a sound and wondering how smart it is to step on Satanael's tail when he squeezes his ass right behind me.

Eric, his back pressed on the large trunk of a tree across from me, gives me an infuriating grin. I glare at him.

His grin grows impossibly wide.

"Dude you really need to knock it off." Hissing quietly, I wiggle to get more room for myself.

"I shall knock Mammon off when we find him." No clue why I'm whispering when Satanael's voice will wake the dead up. A shiver crawls up my spine when he speaks right in my ear.

"Instead of doing a monster rush through Hell, you could've found him long before now."

Huffing in annoyance I stick my head out and check to see if Raphael is coming back. He is the leanest among all three men, so he is our scouting party. Narsi is sulking somewhere behind us because I made him stop biting my father. When nothing but forest meets my eyes, I duck back in my hiding spot.

"If you found him, we would've had less problems now." Continuing my lecture, I rub the hilt of the dagger with my fingers. I miss my dagger, the one that felt like it was as much a part of me as my arms or legs.

"You have lost your weapon." The expectant way Satanael says that makes me zero in on his face.

"I did, yeah. But I was too busy dying to think about grabbing it." Seeing him flinch stabs me in the chest, but I manage to grind my teeth. Can he read my mind? I was just thinking that.

His burning gaze flicks to my hand where the pads of my fingers are still rubbing the hilt. He either reads minds, or he is too observant for my good. Sucking in a sharp intake of breath, I press my back to the tree behind me, my spine hurting from the way I mold into it. A blade is shoved in my face, and Satanael's hand is the one holding it.

My heart jumps in my throat trying to choke me, and my father's face gets bathed in a golden glow. He jerks back, shock written all over his face even though his hand doesn't lower. Flicking my eyes to the sharp edge too close to my neck, I do a double take, the air gushing through my lips when I see him holding my dagger. The golden glow disappears, the sight of my weapon erasing everything else from my mind.

"I picked it up that night ... before I left." The pause in his words is when he swallows thickly, and the pain I feel twists my stomach.

"Thank you," I murmur, not taking my eyes off it.

Gingerly, I reach my hand out and take it from him. When the weight settles in my palm, warmth spreads through me, and it's so much it makes me lightheaded. I never thought I'd see it again. My gaze flicks to Eric and I see him watching us with a small smile on his face. He gives me an encouraging nod.

"I'm surprised you can handle it." I roll it in my hand, marveling at having to hold it. "Eric couldn't."

"Of course I can handle it." The arrogance I know too well comes out loud and clear, and I can't help but smile as I lift my gaze to his face. "It has my essence in it. It is a part of me as much as it is a part of you. Shadow can't hold it because of your mother's essence. Not many from Hell can."

"But you can."

"Only because it is mixed with mine." Giving me a rueful grin, he shrugs a tiny twitch of one shoulder. "I can still rub it in his face."

"Right." Snickering, I turn to see Eric glowering at Satanael.

Giggling under my breath, I replace the borrowed

dagger with mine in the holster on my thigh. The other one goes on my other side where leather straps wrap around my leg. It'll have to do for now. Two weapons are better than one with Mammon's confrontation vastly approaching.

"I'm glad you came to your senses earlier." The words are out before I can stop them. "It would've been a shame if you had to die."

If I surprise him, he doesn't show it. Watching me intently, he searches my face and I let him. Keeping my gaze steady on his, I let him find whatever he is looking for. What I say is the truth. There is no doubt in my mind that he wouldn't have been the last one standing in that clearing where Narsi lead him to find us.

"I did not try to kill them." It's a simple statement, and there's not a trace of arrogance or gloating in his words.

"Then why fight them at all?" Tilting my head, I frown at him. "It was Narsi that found you. That should've been enough to let you know it was me. Seeing Raphael and Eric with me was just a bonus."

"The djinn will have a hard time pretending they are you. You are impulsive and unpredictable at the best of times. Unless they hold someone you care about over your head. I didn't think you were a djinn. The Archangel and Shadow are a different story. I only wanted to make sure it wasn't a trap." With those words, his gaze falls on Eric standing across from us. I know Eric can hear us since his hearing is better than a human's, and when they nod at each other, I think there must be some silent conversation happening between them.

"You were willing to die to see if it was a trap?" Rubbing my forehead, I try and fail to see his logic.

"The two of them couldn't kill me, djinn or not." Satanael smirks.

"But I could." Now it's my turn to watch him squirm.

"And you would've." Since he didn't phrase it as a question, I don't answer him. Instead, I keep my unwavering eyes on his.

His lips twitch before spreading into a full-blown smile that sends my stomach flipflopping. He brings his hand up and cups my face, mindful of his long claws. Those sharp edges that could cut my face off with a flick of his wrist glide gently over my cheekbone in a caress. The harsh lines on his face soften as he gazes at me.

"Of course you would've. And it makes me proud that you are my blood."

"You are a weirdo." Fighting the tears clogging my throat, I try to make a joke. "No one gets excited knowing they would've been killed."

"It's the perk of being the Devil." He grins and winks at me as his hand disappears from my face.

My chuckle is cut short when Raphael bursts from the foliage panting. Leaves and twigs stick out from his hair and wings, his golden eyes wide on his face. His head swivels around in search of us and I scramble from my spot just as Eric steps out from behind the tree. Raphael's face is practically glowing with glee, all his white teeth gleaming.

"I found him, and he is not alone."

Chapter Twenty-Eight

RAPHAEL

"We can just attack," Helena says for the fifth time, her lips pressed in a firm line.

"We are not sure if that's all of them." I point out to her.

Crouched next to Helena, I count the demons in front of us. There are easily over twenty of them spread out. I have no doubt Mammon has heard that Helena is in the realm. I should've prevented her from allowing that female demon to go around telling everyone she is searching for Satanael. Too late to fix it now, though.

"Are we going to back out if there are more?" Stubbornly, she turns to Satanael and Eric in hopes they will back her up. "No? So we should just go and kill them all."

"So bloodthirsty, my daughter." Satanael chuckles and I join him. She does sound as bloodthirsty as a she-devil, as Colt likes to call her.

"I can't just sit here watching his stupid face. I want to wipe that smirk off it"—Growling, she clenches her teeth—"with my dagger."

"You'll have your chance, Hel." Eric looks like he doesn't know if he should hold her back or let her fight.

I shake my head subtly at him. That male will get the wrath of Satanael's daughter on his head if he says a word. I know it, and he knows it too. A muscle twitches in his jaw when he flicks his gaze at me. At least he gives a jerky nod, although he doesn't look happy about it.

"I don't know why Narsi decided to shrink. The stupid thing could've just eaten his face. Now he sulks around like I took his favorite toy when we need him to be a badass." Huffing in frustration, she hasn't taken her eyes off Mammon.

I agree.

"He is a protective spirit, Helena. He grew that size because he reacts to your power. The stronger you are, the larger he can be. I do not know what the fates have in store for you, but I don't question it anymore," Satanael says thoughtfully, making me turn to him and forget all about Mammon. "The Haltija grew that night because you were at your peak, brimming with power that you couldn't contain. He adapted to keep everyone that tried to hurt you away. I knew there was a reason Zedkiel asked me to bind one for you. I did it no questions asked."

"How did she know that Narsi would find Helena?" Frowning, I push away the uneasy feeling drumming in my gut. "Did the Trowe plan on going through the portal to find her?"

"Narsi was on that path when me and Eric came across him because he was looking for me. He expected me to be there ... in Hell." Demons forgotten, Helena stares at Satanael wide eyed. So am I for that matter.

"I only bound the Haltija to protect you. Your mother gave him instructions on what he has to do. I haven't seen him, not until you found me." Scratching at his chin, Satanael narrows his eyes. "I should've asked more questions I suppose."

"Good luck with that," Eric pipes in, and Helena glares at him. "What? Like you give me any explanation when I ask. Stop growling Eric. Don't scare them Eric. No, because I said so." Eyebrows crawling up his forehead, he dares her to negate him. I almost laugh when her lips whiten and press together without a word.

"Something bigger than all of us is at play. Let us be grateful we are all here now." The guilt is strong inside me, but I decide to push it away. I cannot change what has happened. "As Satanael said, he didn't question it. I didn't question it either when she asked for my oath to protect you. All that lead to this moment."

We all turn to scan our surroundings, lost in thoughts of our own. Can it be true? Did Zedkiel know all of this was going to happen? Did she set everything in motion long before Helena was even born? And did she know I would sacrifice my place in Heaven by stepping foot in Purgatory? Because there is no going back for me now. No portal to Heaven will allow my shadowed soul to pass. If Helena didn't need my protection anymore, it would've been a greater mercy if they left me there. I can barely feel the connection to my home now, just a slight echo of what used to be a beautiful song in my veins. I grip my knees to stop my hands from shaking. It's too late to think on it now. I don't regret my actions, but what does it mean that Purgatory didn't hold me there? It was a life for a life, yet all of us are here.

"You okay?" A small hand is placed over mine, fingers wrapping gently around it. Helena is watching me with a worried look on her face.

"Of course." She doesn't believe my forced smile. "Just an old man thinking about times past. What do humans call it? Nostalgia."

"Right." She rolls her eyes at me. "I almost believed you there, but luckily for you we have shit to do." With one last squeeze, she removes her hand from mine, taking the comfort she offers with it. "I'll drill you later and you'll spill your guts, I promise. Let's kill this asshole first."

"I say we just attack. I can take more than half of them on my own," Satanael snarls, already poising up to spring.

I give everything one last look before I agree with him. They are a bunch of higher-ranking demons, but they still aren't a match for Eric or him. I might have a harder time because the power from after Helena used me as a puppet is more than half drained after my fight with Satanael.

"The two of you can go first. I'll stay around Helena to keep anyone that slips through you away from her." All three of them look at me strangely, but I stare ahead keeping my shoulders back like this is some strategy and not another of my shortcomings.

"I'll feel better if he is close now that Narsi is nowhere to be found." Helena shocks me by going along with my plan. "It's a good plan as long as you leave a piece of Mammon for me. I really, really want to stab him between his horns."

"That can be arranged." Eric chuckles, but still throws his calculating looks my way.

"Actually," Helena lifts off her knees, turning her back on all of us before we have time to see what she is doing. "I have a better idea."

With one glance and a fast grin thrown at us over her shoulder, she straightens up, raising her chin defiantly. Eric scrambles forward and reaches for her arm, but she bolts out of the thick shrubbery, leaving his fingers to curl around empty air. Satanael snarls a curse, and I swear up a storm right along with him, fumbling to stand up and follow her. The woman is trouble personified. Even her father cannot match the mischief she makes regardless if humans call him the Devil or not.

We all burst from our hiding spot one after another, skidding to a stop. Every demon in sight is staring, their mouths gaping open, and that includes Mammon. Helena is a few steps in front of us, her hip cocked to the side and her hand placed coquettishly on it. With her shoulders thrown back, her head turns from side to side as she looks at everyone facing her. At least until she locks eyes with Mammon because the fury on his face is palpable.

"Hey motherfuckers. Here I am. Let's get this shitstorm started, shall we?" Pulling her dagger out, she flips it in the air and twirls it between her fingers before pointing it right at Mammon. "Your ugly ass is mine!"

An angry roar splits the air and all of them charge. With a laugh, Eric and Satanael launch themselves at the onslaught, streaks of red and black passing Helena. An incredulous laugh bubbles in my chest and I throw my head back, unable to stop it. When I look her way again, her face is turned to me over her shoulder, her eyes twinkling with mirth and a serene smile gracing her face.

"Let's show these idiots how it's done."

"Let us show them." With a gallant nod at her bravery, I chuckle and follow at her back.

Chapter Twenty-Nine

HELENA

Satanael and Eric collide with the first line of demons sprinting my way. Maybe I should've thought this out better, or at least followed their plan. Waiting for Narsi to get his tiny butt back so he can help may have been smart, too. But the longer I watch Mammon, the more everything he has done so far comes to the surface, and the more I think about all the people I care about that he has hurt in his twisted power game. All of that hits me like a rock, makes me want him dead. Erasing him from every realm and wiping out his existence may not even be enough to placate me.

With Raphael at my back, we reach the fight, claws and horns swinging on all sides around us. Ducking under a thick arm, my dagger slashes wildly at a bare torso wide enough to block my view. The runes come to life on the blade, red and gold dancing in the night and parting the skin with ease. The demon screams, a high-pitched sound that does not belong on a creature as large as him. His head rears as his face twists into an ugly mask filled with hatred, and he aims his long horns at my chest. Thick fingers wrap around it, and Raphael, straining with all his might, stops the sharp tip from impaling me where I stand. Muscles bulging on his arms, he wrenches the demon back by bending him in half. Lifting my arm over my head, I slam my weapon to the hilt in the hollow of the creature's throat. Black blood coats my fingers, and I almost lose the grip I have on my dagger. Tightening my hold, I release a squelching sound as I pull it out. He crumbles on the ground between the Archangel and me, almost crushing my toes with his huge head.

"Watch out." Raphael shoves me back, both his hands taking hold of an axe that is flung at my head.

Stumbling back, I catch myself so I don't end up on my ass, bending my knees and barely avoiding the claws slashing at my back. It's too crowded to see, and the demons are doing their best to overwhelm us with their numbers. Pivoting, I press my back to Raphael's, my forearm screaming in pain when I block a creature's fist, stopping it just in time so it doesn't put a dent in my skull. Teeth grinding, my other hand shoots out and jabs the dagger in his upper arm before I yank it down with all I've got. My ears are ringing from the furious roar coming from it, but he pulls back and gives my arm a break. I'm not sure I could've held his strength back much longer.

Snarls and outraged shrieks are a constant buzz, Raphael's body bumping at my back with every move he makes the only thing keeping me grounded in the fray. Two demons charge at me from both sides, lips curled over sharp teeth on their anger-twisted faces. A jolt goes through me, numbing my head when claws arch down at me, leaving me with no way of stopping them both. If I move, they'll shred the Archangel's back or wings. If I don't, they'll rip me to pieces. Unwilling to be the reason Raphael dies, a scream is ripped out of my chest and I swing wildly, twirling on the balls of my feet. My arm is almost pulled out of its socket when the dagger hits resistance, my shoulder and back burning in pain when I feel the skin ripping like fabric coming undone at the seams. I guess I didn't avoid all of the razor-sharp claws.

The ground under my feet tilts violently, my head jerking back when a chunk of hair gets tangled in something ripping it out. My boot hits a bump, pitching me even more sideways than the trembling of the earth. Flailing my arms, I try to keep my balance and stay on my feet. Not releasing the grip on my dagger, another pained cry from me overshadows the cacophony of sound.

The world around me explodes.

My stomach empties, a feeling that sends my heart kicking painfully against my ribs. Panicked shouts reach my ears, Eric's roar louder than any of them. My father's wrath-filled scream curdles the blood in my veins just as a hand grabs me, stopping my fall half an inch from the blood-soaked ground. The tip of my nose is almost touching the wet puddle, its stench burning my nostrils. With my hair draping over my face, I can see nothing, and being blind makes all the noises around me more terrifying, especially since I can only guess what I will find when I regain my sight. My knees buckle when I'm lifted and pressed to a warm chest. Recognizing Raphael's arm holding me up around my waist, I sag against him, flipping my hair back so I can see once more.

"I got you," the Archangel rasps, unable to hide the worry in his voice.

"Thank …" my words trail off.

The hand that is pushing my hair away slowly falls to my side with a tremor. My fingers spasm around the hilt of my dagger, eyes going wide at what is revealed to me now that I can see. Raphael tightens his hold, pulling me closer to him, his body as rigid as an unyielding stone. Eric and Satanael have somehow reached us, standing half a step in front of us with their waists bent slightly and arms to their sides as they hold everyone back. The gap between them is enough to short-circuit my brain.

Four djinn stand up facing us, Mammon in the center of them with a gloating grin on his stupid face. The demons that were attacking us are inching closer to them, leaving an empty circle around us like the makeshift arena of an illegal fight. *How appropriate*, the voice in my head says, sounding as weak as I feel.

"Well." Mammon claps his hands, rubbing them together excitedly. "Now that everyone we need is here, let us end this once and for all."

"Mammon, I will feast on your flesh and drink every drop of blood from your ripped throat." Satanael snarls, the venom in his voice raising all the short hairs on my body.

"Ah, but you'll have to be able to win for that to happen, Satanael. From where I'm standing, your days are numbered. This is where all of you die." Wariness creeps over Mammon's face but it's gone in a blink, too fast for me to be sure I didn't imagine it. "I must say, having Lucifer's first born was not what I expected but that just makes this so much better. I love seeing him broken."

Eric doesn't make a sound, and not even a muscle twitches on his body. My heart shrivels for him, but I have no strength to reach out and touch him. It takes all the energy inside me just to breathe and not faint. Dark spots are dancing at the corners of my eyes, the skin on my back where I'm pressed to Raphael burning so bad I'm sure I'll miss our deaths because I'll black out.

"Breathe Helena." Raphael's words are just a breath in my ear, and I fill my lungs with stinking air. "Just breathe."

"You have always been good at talking, Mammon." The conversational way Eric says that contradicts the horrifying sound of his voice. Not even my father has managed to numb me in fear like that. "In all your planning"—Eric's large hand waves nonchalantly, encompassing everyone around us—"you forgot one very important thing."

"Do share it before you die, Shadow." Mammon leans forward eagerly with a crazed glint in his black eyes, and his lips pull back in an evil smile, revealing rows of razor teeth.

"Lucifer likes to follow his own rules, believe it or not." The amusement in Eric's voice is abruptly cut off with his next words. "I am not my father."

Raphael chuckles, shocking the shit out of me. "And so it begins." He breathes the words.

"Let us dance, Mammon." Satanael laughs, spreading his arms wide as if he wants to embrace everyone.

All hell breaks loose, literally.

Chapter Thirty

HELENA

Lifting one arm over his head, Satanael drops on his knees and rams it on the ground with a resounding boom. The earth ripples like a restless wave in an ocean before fractures crackle and spread fast in front of him. As they reach Mammon's feet the floor opens, spreading apart and creating gaping, bottomless holes that are like hungry beasts as they devour screaming demons in their depths. Island, or piece of land forms between the open darkness just as bright flames shoot up reaching for the sky. Everything gets bathed in red and orange, and the heat from it tightens my skin.

The arm holding me standing up disappears from my waist and I lock my knees to stay upright. Eric, Satanael, and Raphael lift in the air with a powerful swoosh of their wings, looking ominous in the raging inferno around us. My mouth drops open when thick shadows—and no doubt so solid I can touch them if I reach out with my fingers—twist and surround the djinn and Mammon. My hands are shaking, my breath shuddering in my lungs when rage-filled roars come out of our enemies.

Mammon unfurls his wings as well, straightening to his full height to face us as the djinn float to his sides. Bile rises in my throat from the eager anticipation on their faces as they face the three men willing to die to protect me, to keep me safe and alive while I uselessly stay here surrounded by a cage of dancing flames and watch them. Will I still stand here if they lose their lives one by one? Am I really worth that much?

No. I'm not.

That answer screams through my mind, making my blood boil with the same wrath that runs through my father's veins. Anger as thick as Eric's shadows clogs my throat so much it chokes me. The righteousness that beats with each pump of Raphael's blood fuels the insanity overtaking my mind. They will not die to protect me. I will not let them.

My head snaps back, face raising to the sky as a scream that makes my ears bleed is ripped from my chest. It shreds my throat and my insides and is filled with rage, pain, and so much fear for their lives. Arms thrown back, I stare at the empty sky, the sound of my voice continuing so long I have no idea how because there's no air left in my lungs.

Blasts of power hit me, feeling like a breeze on my skin when bodies collide midair. The burning of my back intensifies into pain so crippling I should be on the ground, yet I keep my feet planted on the ground, staying frozen like a sacrifice spread to the worlds. My head moves slowly, trails of blood from my ears soaking my neck and hair. Heat builds behind my eyes as I watch Eric twirl in the air, all power and anger with his teeth bared in a snarl that shreds skin off the djinn. The shadows pulse around him, holding those creatures down for his deadly claws and horns. Blood covers his arms and chest, his powerful wings beating the air with punishing swoops.

On the other side, Satanael has a djinn in his jaw, teeth clamped tight as he shakes his head like a dog with a bone. His own claws are tearing the skin on the djinn's chest into ribbons, blood showering his form while the creature flops lifelessly around him. The triangular tip of his tail flicks restlessly at his back before shooting up and impaling the djinn.

Raphael is locked with another djinn, his arms straining to hold the monster back, gold and green power snaking over them and melting the djinn's skin wherever it touches it. His right wing opens wide, swinging down harshly and flinging another djinn away from him. A shadow falls over me, my head snapping in the direction it comes from. Mammon grins at me from above my head, and a sense of calm washes over me as the powerful but strange pulse thumps in the center of my chest.

I smile.

Disgust twists Mammon's face and his lips pull back over his teeth. Angling his body down, he swoops in on me, claws outstretched like a vulture ready to catch his prey. I stand still, holding my breath while I wait for what is to come next. The tension leaves my body as he nears, my fingers tightening around the hilt of my dagger pressing against my thigh. Mammon's black eyes glitter like obsidians, the flames reflecting on the shiny surface. When he gets within reach, I take a step back and force him to come closer. My arm shoots out, the runes on the dagger flaring bright before it parts the skin on his stomach and splits him open from hip to chest.

With an outraged cry, he jolts back, his foot catching me

in the shoulder with so much force my feet elevate off the ground. My eyes widen in shock, the unexpected tilt of my perception allowing me to see one of his wings catch the flames that spread over him. He screams again, flapping wildly as I'm pitched back so far, I pass through the ring of fire surrounding me. There is only a moment where I stand suspended in space before my stomach drops and gravity pulls me in the hungry depths of the bottomless hole. A swirl of white disturbs the fires.

My neck snaps back, body jolting when a grip on my ankle stops my fall. Back hitting the side of the open earth with a tooth jarring thump, I can't stop myself from biting my tongue. Blood fills my mouth. Gasping for air, I lift my head and look up my body to see Narsi holding onto my foot with both hands, flames burning the curls off his head. He doesn't seem to notice. Yellowed teeth grinding and his skin blistering over his tiny body, he pulls with everything he's got. With strength he shouldn't possess, he heaves me up, his wrinkled, scrunched-up, eyeless face disappearing from view.

"Narsi, watch out!" my scream comes too late.

Mammon swoops down, kicking my sidekick with a foot to his head. Narsi is flung forward, his body rolling over my head. The free fall feeling empties my insides as I follow him down, his tiny fingers still holding my ankle. My hair streams past my face and I close my eyes, acceptance pushing away the fear that is trying to choke me. I only hope with me being gone that Eric, Raphael, and my father will get to live. It should be a good enough sacrifice for whoever the asshole was that created our destinies. It's the only thing I've got to hold onto as I face my end.

Because this is the end.

I know deep in my bones there will be no coming back

from this. Not even to fight off dozens of people wearing my face, not djinn or power-hungry Fallen. It will just be me, the abomination that creates chaos through all the realms, snuffed from existence. The abnormality erased from the thread of life.

I realize the air that is rushing past my ears has quieted and the heat on my skin from the shooting flames no longer burns my skin. I feel weightless, suspended in silence. Just Narsi's grip on my leg the only indication I'm not alone. Reluctantly I open my eyes, blinking so fast my brain can't understand what I'm seeing.

"Hello, Helena."

An old woman stands above me, head tilted to the side as she watches me with curiosity in her white, glowing eyes. A slight smile lifts the corners of her mouth, making the wrinkles of her delicate face even more prominent. Her features flicker, changing from a young girl's to a middle-aged woman's, then to the old face that I first see. I keep blinking, dumbfounded with no clue what to do.

"I'll eat her face." Narsi's hiss jerks me from the stunned state.

Chapter Thirty-One

HELENA

"What?" Scrambling up, I snatch the crazy Trowe in the air when he jumps at the woman. "You're not eating anyone."

I have no idea who this is but the power coming off her is enough to make me want me to curl up in a ball, rocking and whimper to comfort myself. My body feels heavy when I climb on my knees, clutching my wiggling sidekick to my chest. The woman doesn't move, watching us both like insects under her feet. With great effort, I plant one boot firmly under me, pushing up on my feet. I hobble to my feet and stand, coming face to face with her since we are the same height. Weight presses on my shoulders so suddenly my mouth opens in a silent O. I topple over, the back of my head smacking into something with a thud and causing Narsi to sprawl on my chest.

The woman chuckles.

Her face pops into view and I blink owlishly at her. Even Narsi is quiet and not wiggling. He's probably as stunned as I am. The old lady grins at me, displaying rows of even, white teeth.

"Ouch!" The sharp pain in my back jerks me to the side, which flings the Trowe off me.

Glaring at him, I roll on my hands and knees, stopping when Narsi raises his hand that's holding a golden feather, his fingers gripping it like a torch in front of him. He stares at it in awe.

So do I.

"Where did you get that?" I try to snatch it off him, but he scrambles away on his knees. "And who are you?" Still sending pissed-off glances at the dumbass, I turn to the woman. "Where am I?"

"It is not important who I am, but who *you* are, Helena." The sound of her voice makes me sigh.

"Who am I then?" Stiffening when I notice the affect she has on me, I take a step away from her and topple over again, the weight on my back pulling me down.

"What the hell is wrong with me?" Frustrated, I sit up and crane my neck in attempt to see how badly I'm injured since I can't stay upright.

Screaming, I jump up.

"Wings!" Shrieking, I pull a Narsi and run in place in a circle as if I can see them better. "I have fucking wings!"

The golden appendages move slightly up and down in sync with my shoulders. Getting dizzy from my insane chasing-a-tail stunt, I stop swaying on my feet. Something tickles my leg and I glance down thinking Narsi creeped up to cling to me like he usually does. A thick tendril tries to coil around my shin, so I kick my foot to shake it off. Something brushes my tailbone and my ass cheeks clench.

I freeze.

With eyes so wide they may pop out of my sockets, I stare at the lady. Warily, my arm moves at a snail's pace and reaches behind me. It passes through soft feathers until my fingers gingerly probe at the tail sticking out of my butt. My ass cheeks clench again at the sensation.

"Oh, my God," I breathe the words through numb lips. Narsi snickers like an idiot.

"You are surprised." The woman cocks her head in a very inhuman way, almost like a bird. Honestly, it's creepy as hell.

"You think?" My mouth closes with a snap as soon as I spit the words at her.

"This is who you are." Her hand moves slowly up and down, indicating the freak show I'm turning out to be. "The wrath of the Devil, and the Mercy of God. Did you not know?"

"I was that without the extra limbs, too." Realizing I'm still strangling my tail, I snatch my hand back.

"You have a choice to make, child." Goosebumps raise on my arms and legs when three voices come out of her mouth at the same time.

"Why am I here?" Eyes darting left and right, I inch back to look for a way out of wherever this place is.

"Would you rather have died?"

The fog around us swirls and I take a step forward when it opens like a screen revealing Eric, Satanael, and Raphael still fighting. The hair is plastered on their heads, blood running down their bodies from their many open wounds. One of Eric's wings hangs lower than the other. Why do all these assholes go for his wings first. My teeth grind with a crunch.

"Can you send me back?" I force my eyes away from the men. "Please?" Unshed tears clog my throat.

"Perhaps." Her unconcerned tone pisses me off, but I hold my tongue. "Depends on what you choose."

"Let's hear it." Urgency stabs me in the chest.

"So eager." Her smile is like the cat that ate the canary and it sends a shiver rolling down my spine. "Ah, youth is such a beautiful thing. Stupid, but beautiful nonetheless."

"The choice." Swallowing thickly, I ball my hands into fists. "Let's hear it."

"Your life was mine." The blood chills in my veins when those glowing eyes turn their full intensity on my face. "An Archangel and a Prince of Hell traded their own in exchange."

My mouth opens and closes but nothing comes out.

"Yet all three of you were freed." Tsking like we have tried to trick her, she wiggles a finger in my face. I shrink back from it like it's a snake. "A sacrifice has to be made." Offering a barely perceptible shrug, she starts to circle me. "It's the way of things, you see."

"What … what do you want?" My voice breaks but I manage to push the words out.

"The Archangel, or Lucifer's son." Coming to a stop in front of me, she grins, her face flickering again.

"No." The word is ripped from me as my knees give out, making me drop in front of her. "No!" Sobs are wrenched from the bottom of my soul. "I'll never choose."

She stands still, not saying a word as I cry at her feet. Those damn wings curl around me like a blanket. I hate them. I hate everything, including her—whoever she is—for asking me to pick one of the men that will give their life without a thought in exchange for mine. Rage hotter than Satanael's wrath explodes in my chest.

"You can't have them," screaming in her face, I jump to my feet. "I'll die before I let you have one of them."

My arm swings, the dagger I grip clutched tight in it. It sails right for her throat, but she moves so fast I flip around wildly to see her standing at my back. A frown scrunches her face before she rights herself.

"Or your power." At her mumbled words, my hand drops to my side.

"Have it." She rocks back on her heels at my outburst. "Take it. It's yours. Just leave them alone."

"You will be nothing but a human. Easily broken and easily killed."

"Have it." Repeating it with more conviction then anything I've ever said, I wait.

"You cannot have Lucifer's son as a mate if you are human." Her eyes widen in anticipation and something inside me dies.

I will lose Eric. *But he will be alive*, my ripped to shreds heart whispers.

"Have it," I choke out, fat tears spilling down my cheeks.

Her eyes widen comically and she gapes at me. Pissed off, I thrust both arms at her and that makes her stumble back.

"Have it!"

"I knew you would prove worthy." A proud grin spreads on her face, and it confuses the shit out of me.

"We are the Fates," three voices boom, the power behind them dropping me on my knees. "You shall keep the balance of the realms in our name. The Archangel Raphael will be bound to your life. Lucifer's son will be bound to your heart. If you fail, you will answer to us. Your life will be ours to do as we see fit."

Heat slams into my chest and flips me back. I'm actually shocked my spine doesn't break. I'm burning. My whole body is on fire, my mouth open in a silent scream but there is nothing I can do to stop it. I watch the woman bend at

173

the waist as her face comes so close to mine that I feel her breath on my skin. A scent I can't name fills my lungs, and it's so beautiful tears run down my face. She whispers in my ear, her words numbing my brain. The pain feels like it lasts for an eternity until the silence that is plugging my ears disappears with a pop.

Everything returns with a whoosh.

"Hel." Eric's voice jerks my head up.

I'm standing in the forest, the ground still split open and flames still jumping at the sky. The djinn are gone, their bodies flung all over the place. Eric is standing to my left peering down at me with worry on his face. He's never looked more beautiful to me, horns and claws included.

"Helena?" I turn to my right to see Raphael, fear and relief clouding his angelic face as he reaches for me.

His white wings are covered in blood, his chest oozing blood from many wounds. Yet he is worried about me. I want to scream and yell at the skies. I want to get my hands on the woman I have no doubt fucks with us like this. Then I remember her words. I'll deal with whatever comes my way as long as she stays away from the two of them.

Satanael is in front of us, holding Mammon down on his knees with a hand pressed to his neck, claws stabbed in his skin. My father stares at me with his mouth open just like Eric and Raphael. Both of Mammon's wings are missing, laying on either side of him. Which reminds me ...

"Umm, I have wings." The golden feathers rustle on my back.

"I can see." Eric sounds as incredulous as I feel.

"And a tail." The said appendage flicks and my ass cheeks clench.

"So we see." Raphael sounds faint but Eric chuckles.

I glare at him. "I met the Fates." Swallowing thickly, I stiffen my spine. "She … or maybe they... anyway, whatever they are, they gave me this."

"We saw," Eric tells me, and I whirl on him.

"You did? How?" I saw them fighting, so there's no way they could see what I was doing right?

"That's what killed the djinn." Satanael grumbles. "We saw she pulled you in but didn't know where she took you." His burning gaze scans me from head to toe. "I was going to burn the realms down if she didn't give you back."

"Never mind." A shiver shakes me just thinking about it. "We are all fine, that's what matters." Fingers tangling in Narsi's hair—that thankfully is back and not burnt—where and with him hanging on my leg, I scan the forest. "How do we go home?"

"The portal is right there." Satanael stabs the finger from his free hand at a clearing not far away that's surrounded by rocks with runes on them.

"Leave it to the Devil to point a way out of Hell," Eric pipes in with humor.

"What shall I do with this one?" Satanael shakes the snarling Mammon.

Remembering some of the words the lady whispered in my ear, I raise up in the air, the flying coming as natural as breathing even though it boggles my mind. Eric and Raphael do the same and we close in on the asshole that started this mess.

"We should keep him imprisoned somewhere," Raphael says reluctantly. "Spare his life but make sure he never does anything like this again."

"I say we rip the fucker limb from limb. A shit like him should die slowly," Eric growls, arguing his point.

I snort.

"What?" My father lifts an eyebrow at my snickering.

"I never thought I'd say this, but I literally have an angel and a demon on my shoulders."

Eric and Raphael both bark out a laugh at the same time. Satanael grins devilishly at me. Even Narsi joins them. Only Mammon glares at me with hatred burning in his gaze. The words the woman said to me echo in my head. *You must kill Mammon to keep them both. It's a mercy for his tortured soul and a price I'm willing to take in turn.*

Gulping down the unease of killing a restrained creature, I look at everyone around me. *It's worth it*, I tell myself, shaking off the doubt and recalling everything and everyone the asshole has killed already in his quest for power.

"I made him a promise tonight." Gripping the dagger, I lift it above my head. Mammon's eyes widen and I grin at him. "Playtime, motherfucker." The runes burst with light as the dagger sinks hilt deep into his skull right between his eyes. His body drops, sliding off the blade with a squelch. I blow out a breath.

"Let's go home." Placing the blood-coated dagger in the sheath on my thigh, I take Eric's hand in mine on one side, and Raphael's on my other. They give me a reassuring squeeze of my fingers and warmth spreads through me. They are safe. The last words of the woman whisper through my ears.

"Your mother lives."

My heart lurches at the thought but I'm not sure that I actually heard her say that, or she said your mother believed. My body was being pulled away from her and I could've been imagining things. Regardless, I have no intention of worrying about it, or even giving it a second thought. I don't care. I'm alive. Eric and Raphael are alive. I don't need anything more than that.

Satanael opens the portal and gives me a proud grin. "I shall see you soon, daughter."

"Don't rush, Devil. I could use a bit of a break from Hell, family or not." He chuckles at my words while reclining his head regally. We enter the portal and a weight settles on my leg.

"I ate his face." A groan comes out of my chest at Narsi's words. Eric and Raphael chortle.

"Just another day in Helena's life," I say with a sigh as we disappear through the portal, my father's laugh echoing from behind us.

Betrayal, secrets, and a whole lot of Hell. What could possibly go wrong?

I'm the Devil's daughter, and peace? Not in my vocabulary. My past is a tangled mess of betrayal and power plays, and Eric's not doing me any favours. The Fates are at it again, and the truth? It's gonna cost me everything. Even my soul.

Turn the page for a free preview…

Give a Devil His Due: Chapter One

HELENA

I failed.

Miserably and absolutely failed, and not just humanity but myself and everyone I love. How's that for a wake up call? The gray sky permanently scowling in my direction and the jutting remains of the destroyed city of Atlanta reaching for it mock me without regret. Tightening the hold around my knees, I press them harder to my chest like that will lighten the crushing guilt squeezing my lungs and preventing me from taking a full breath. The only good thing that comes from it is that it stops my body from shaking at times like this when the pain is too much to bear.

"You cannot hide here forever, Helena." Raphael's voice comes as a murmur from behind me.

Not having a reaction to the sudden sound might come as a surprise to the Archangel, but I know he has been standing there hiding in the shadows for almost an hour. That's all he has done since we returned from Purgatory. Stalks me like he expects me to fall apart or lose my shit without warning.

"I can try." A heavy sigh trembles through my numb lips, and I twist my head to look at him over my shoulder. "Might as well join me, Raphael, and speak your peace. We both know Eric will find my hidey hole sooner rather than later. Both of you are proving to be a pain in my ass lately."

"Maybe if you talk to us, we won't worry as much about your state of mind." Rooftiles crack and shift under his boots when he gingerly moves to where I'm perched on top of the safe house. With a wary look around, he lowers his tall frame, his arm brushing mine when he plops down. "It's not just you who has all of us on edge. Your emotions affect the Trowe, as well. The last thing we need is to lose control of the spirit and him destroying whatever is left of the city."

It's been few days since we returned, and I still can't get over what I found. In the middle of the fight, things didn't look that bad around me. Stupidly, I thought we would win this war with the jinn if I sacrificed myself. Because that's what they wanted, wasn't it? To remove the abomination so things could be balanced. Instead, it turned out I, of all things, *am* the balance, and those assholes want chaos to rule so they can seize control of Heaven and Hell.

My breathing sounds too loud in the silence surrounding me and Raphael on the roof. "You don't need to worry about Narsi or me. We will do whatever is necessary to fix this mess." My hand flips around, encompassing the destroyed world before our eyes. "All of this is my fault." Pretending I don't notice the side-eyed glance he throws my way, I keep my eyes locked on the plumes of smoke cousring up from parts of Atlanta where the hunters are burning whatever bodies they can find.

Not many of the hunters are left standing, either. The ones we can spare are standing guard at the still-open portals in case additional monsters poke their cursed heads out and join their brethren in the human realm in order to erase it from existence. I'd like to blame them for being dumb and guided by their evil, bloodthirsty mindsets, but it's not like I'm better than them. The fact that if the human realm falls it'll destroy Heaven and Hell has never stopped me from making idiotic, selfish decisions. Maybe it will be for the best if everything goes to shit and time resets itself. Whatever new humans, angels, and demons are created might make better choices than we ever will.

The faces of those lost float in my mind's eye, taunting me and souring the taste in my mouth. My best friend—along with the man who raised me as his own child despite what it meant for him with the Order—my other friends succumbing to the jinn, and the demons trying to make a living away from the hatred the Archangels and Archdemons fanned all flicker one face after another until my head spins, and I clutch it between my hands.

"Hel." Raphael's hand is a warm and solid weight on my shoulder, pulling me back from the madness I'm drowning in. "Thinking of what could've been or should've been will change nothing."

"You mean I shouldn't feel like the lowest piece of shit for causing the apocalypse?" Laughter bursts from me, cold and unhinged. "I should brush it off all the lives that were lost so I could sit here and watch humanity die off. You are right, we should have a party because I lived."

Tears burn the back of my eyes, but I refuse to let them fall. Everyone who died does not need me crying. No amount of tears will bring them back or give any meaning to their deaths. I should've cried before they were lost. Maybe if I did better, if I made different decisions, they could've lived even if I was no longer among them. Too many maybes and not enough tears to absolve me from my sins. Everything in me quieted with Raphael's next words.

"Let me not pray to be sheltered from dangers, but to be fearless in facing them." His fingers move a strand of my hair, tucking it behind my ear when I turn my head to face him. The sad smile on his face burns in my chest like a dagger being twisted there. "Let me not beg for the stilling of my pain, but for the heart to conquer it."

"Quoting Tagore should make me feel better for all I've done?" My snort forms a line between his brows, and for the first time, I see the turmoil brewing in his golden eyes. "We did this Raphael. Well, *I* did this, and the rest of you followed in some dumb quest to protect me and keep me alive. For what exactly? How is my life worth more than theirs?"

"My Father has a plan for all of us, Helena. Even when we don't understand it, it's best not to fight it. I'm sure things will become clear ... eventually." His pep talk would be more convincing if he didn't look like he didn't believe his own words. I was happy to enlighten him on that little fact.

"Like Michael going missing? Let's not forget Lucifer." Tapping a finger on my lips, I pretend like I'm thinking about it. "Oh, right. Satanael being chained like a dog or my mother being killed played integral parts in that plan, too. I think I see the bigger picture now. You are absolutely right. There must be a superior plan in the works, and all the humans were just sacrifices in some cosmic ritual for a better future to please the Devine."

"Hel—"

"You should've left me there, Raphael." His sharp intake of breath should make me to shut up, but it doesn't.

"If it was me they wanted, it would've been a worthy sacrifice to save humanity."

"How dare you spit on everything we have done." Raphael unfolds to his full height until an Archangel is looming over me instead of the man I know. "We all pay penance for our actions, and all of us have lost too much to give up now. Faith is all some of us have left, and I'll be damned if I let you take that away by dwelling on memories of how things should've been." Fists clenching at his sides, he leans forward to lock gazes with me. "So stay here and romanticize about what the world would've been like if you didn't exist, but do it fast, Helena. When you are done living in the past, join us to form a plan for the future—one wearing a cloak of reality, not wishy-washy dreams."

Watching him storm off the roof, I struggle to hold my tears back. With a sigh, I turn to stare at the city, an occasional shout or screech from a dying demon reaching my ears. Raphael is right in everything he said, but I'm not sure I can move on from the memories pressing like a mountain on my chest. If the suffering I inflict on myself doesn't end, I might be a ticking bomb walking among what's left of this world, but that brings another question to mind. If I don't want to look at what's left in my wake, why am I fighting so hard to be here now? Uninvited, a memory I fight so hard to suppress blooms in my head, and it's too loud and too vivid to ignore.

"We are the Fates." Three voices boom, the power behind them dropping me on my knees. "You shall keep the balance of the realms in our name. The Archangel Raphael will be bound to your life. Lucifer's son will be bound to your heart. If you fail, you will answer to us. Your life will be ours to do as we see fit."

My shaking hand pushes the hair falling in my eyes, and I grab a fistful of it as my lids squeeze shut. The sting on my scalp grounds me from the whirlwind of pain and guilt threatening to sweep me under and let me drown. I didn't fight to survive just for myself. It was for Eric and Raphael as well. Another selfish decision on my part, but I can't find it in me to regret that one. There is nothing I wouldn't do for them. *Let's not pretend there is not something else you are trying to avoid, too.* A voice in my head sounding an awful lot like my father's reminds me of things I don't want to voice, and I suck in a breath.

Pushing off the rooftiles, I stand and face broken Atlanta with a new determination. *Your mother lives.* Those words, which I had shoved into the deepest corners of my soul, mock me. Maybe there is a way to fix all the wrongs. Zadkiel, after all, is Mercy of God, right? My mother, if – and that is a huge if to hang my hopes on – she is alive, could change things. Right? Raphael said we need faith, so I just have to believe in that.

A plan forms slowly as I crawl inside the safe house, leaving the destruction behind. Too busy to alleviate my guilt, it never dawns on me why Raphael stormed off the roof instead of flying away like he always does when he gets upset. That should've told me things were worse than I imagined.

But as always, I missed the clues the fates wave in my face.

Give a Devil His Due: Chapter Two

ERIC

"Have you heard back from Maddison?" My grunt turns the question into something my twin brother can make a mockery of.

"If it's too heavy, brother, go work with the rest of the humans. Leave the harder stuff for those of us with enhanced strength and speed." Colt chortles at my glare, while I'm balancing half of a building on my shoulders. "As for our dear cousin, I believe she might be busy making baby demons with Leviathan somewhere on some island. Knowing her, sex is always more important than anything else."

After the tilted wall falls into the foundation and the building rights itself, I dust off my hands and roll my shoulders. No matter how many of them we push back into place, the city stays the same. A deserted place full of dust and smoke. I don't miss the tears Helena tries to hide, nor the pain she pretends not to feel. My mate's nightmares are getting worse, and I need Maddison to help me understand how to help the female I love.

"Don't be a prick, Colt, she will never walk away from a fight. Especially not one that can get all of us killed." Hands on my hips, I turn to search for something else I can fix before the hunters shepherd the humans in need of a shelter this way. "For all we know, they might be imprisoned along with your father."

"Lucifer is your father, too, dear brother." My fingers twitch on my hip with the urge to punch the grin off his face. "But you can go looking for them if it is your wish. I'll make sure your mate is warm and taken care off. What are brothers for if not to help each other out?"

Beating me to is, Beelzebub's meaty fist connects to the side of Colt's head, throwing it back and spinning his body around. My father's confidant proceeds to beat my brother in a whirl of fists and kicks until both of them are a bloody mess sprawled on the dirt and panting for breath.

"Fuck, I needed that." Beelzebub grunts, rolling back on his feet.

"Me, too." Colt joins him, dabbing the back of his hand over his split lip. "I need something to kill, not to crawl over broken buildings and bridges. Don't humans have machines that do these things?"

"George gave the hunters orders to call us when they come across demons or anything not of this world." I ignore his comment about machines. The last thing we need is to make noise some creature will want to investigate when we have no idea what has crawled out in this realm. Yet, I still look at the walkie-talkie hanging from my belt and poke at it like that will make it say something. "Raphael is supervising them, too. I'm sure they'll call for us soon."

"Leave it to the Archangel to lord over everything instead of getting his hands dirty with the rest of us common folk." Colt spits a glob of blood on the ground, his mouth twisting in disgust. "Call the Haltija to do this shit, I'm done. I'll go hunt myself. You coming?" He aims his question to Beelzebub.

Whatever the answer is going to be gets lost in the whoosh of wind that blasts debris and plaster in the air to pelt our skin. Not long behind it, a form casts a shadow over the three of us, blotting whatever weak light the sun is pushing through the clouds of smoke from above Atlanta. It looks like my brother's wishes are manifesting when two more demons join the first one, all of them coming at us fast from the sky.

"All you have to do is ask and ye shall receive," I mutter under my breath as I brace myself for the attack.

"Hell's balls," Colt snorts. "He is starting to sound like Raphael, too. Soon he will sprout white feathers and grow a halo instead of horns."

The demons are of the high classes in Hell, and they hit hard, cutting off any retort I have for my idiot twin. After returning from Purgatory, I learned that any of them left in the human realm were not much for talking or spewing threats at us, unlike when Abaddon was in charge. They attack hard and fight with the desperation of males who need to prove something. Be it their worth or to justify their stupidity for following a loose cannon, I'm not sure, nor do I care. It gives us an outlet to aim our rage at, and that's all that matters.

We fall into a familiar dance of twists and turns, the three of us back-to-back and the demons come at us from all directions, looking for an opening. A coppery scent and the stench of sulfur saturates the air and clogs my nose with each breath I take. Soon it becomes clear we don't want to fight to end it too soon, all of us allowing the feral demons to score hits and shred our skin. Pained grunts and roars echo across the empty street, bouncing off the walls of the buildings we managed to salvage. I'm sure we can drag this out until we tire and then kill the fuckers, but just as I'm thinking that a shrill scream comes from nearby, and it costs me the use of my right arm.

Claws sink into my shoulder, gauging the flesh and shredding my skin. A ferocious roar rips from my chest when the bone is yanked out of its socket, and I lash out wildly at the idiot attacking me. My fist connects to the center of his chest, and his body sails through the air before it hits the wall of the closest building, breaking a hole through it twice as large as he is. So much for salvaging whatever is left of the city.

"Kill them. The humans need our help." Snarling, I grind my teeth and jerk my arm back. The crack of the joint sliding into place sets my teeth on edge and fuels my anger. "Stop playing games before more lives are lost."

"I'm telling you," Colt sneers, ducking to avoid a punch to his face and pummels the demon into a bloody pulp before huffing in annoyance. "Every day he sound more like the Archangel than a Prince of Hell. It's disgusting."

"Your face is disgusting as well, yet I have to look at it daily." Beelzebub sighs, shaking blood and gore from his fingers. "Lead the way, Shadow. The sooner we get to the threat, the less the chances are you'll be Lucifer's only child."

"You are aware that we look alike." Beelzebub grins at my comment when he falls into step with me. "But my guess is, that was your point."

With a shrug, he takes to the sky, and we do too. It's difficult to reach the humans unless you have wings. The streets are either cracked open with craters deep enough to kill whoever falls in them, or they are blocked from crumbled structures that didn't survive the attack the jinn orchestrated. Colt's grumbling follows behind us like an annoying insect refusing to remove itself from the shell of our ears.

"I'm worried about Helena." Not sure what I expect from Beelzebub, but the troubled look crossing his face is not it.

"Let us deal with the scum first."

He and Colt round the corner, leaving me behind to drown in my thoughts. Whatever is down there with the humans is not really a threat to one, little less three of us. The two of them will deal with it much better than I can deal with my own internal demons—the ones inside me that are doing their damn best to drive me insane. My mate needs help, and I'm helpless to aid her.

"Maybe we can all talk to her." I blink Beelzebub into focus, and a frown scrunches my face. How long was I hovering in the air lost in my head? "It was just a handful of rogues. All sorted now." He offers an explanation, misreading my confusion.

"Right." With one last look around, I scrub a hand over my face just as Colt joins us. "We should go back and ..." Glancing between the two of them, I gnaw on my lower lip. "You two can start with the questions. I'll back you up."

"You're too scared to ask your mate if she's losing her shit?" Colt looks too pleased with himself, and I wonder if I can get away with giving him a black eye. Maybe not the best idea before cornering Helena and forcing her to talk, but making him bleed will please me to no end.

"Have you met my mate?" Both of them chuckle and shake their heads like that will embarrass me. "I'm surprised your balls don't shrivel just thinking about making her talk, Colt."

"I have no intention to die this day." My brother adjusts

himself, wincing at the memory. "This was Beelzebub's idea. I'm just a back-up. A back-up who is out of there if there is a dagger in her hand. Don't say I didn't warn you."

"Both of you are pathetic." Beelzebub's bravado would work if he didn't swallow thickly when the safe house comes into view, and Helena disappears inside it from the roof. "I should know not to ask boys to do a man's job."

My feet hit the street as we drop near the front yard, and I roll my shoulders in hopes of removing the tension bunching every muscle on my body. One way or another, I must do this for my mate. She may not appreciate it at the moment, but I know Helena. She will open up if we press her hard enough, and then we will know what is haunting her dreams. Maybe I can't fight an enemy I cannot physically touch, but I sure as hell am willing to give it a try.

I'm still going to keep my mouth shut.

Beelzebub can start the questioning, even if it ends in his funeral.

I love my mate, but I definitely don't have a death wish.

Give a Devil His Due: Chapter Three

HELENA

Well, apart from being a failure, apparently I am a coward as well. Something that becomes abundantly clear the moment I sense Eric getting close to the safe house as I come down from my perch on the roof. I hightail it to the first empty room to hide. Lucky for me, Raphael has taught me how to retract my wings inside my body when I'm not using them, so it's easy to slip away unnoticed. Using my wings is a bit of a stretch, though, since I flop around like a half-dead pigeon a couple of feet above ground before I manage to lift in the air and every landing is with me ending up on my ass, but yeah. What I'm saying is I don't bounce off walls and doors like a pinball machine while I'm walking. The tail is a whole different matter because there is no escaping it. Now I have it wrapped around my waist so I can wear pants, which I ripped at the seam, so the only thing holding them up is my belt. It's a mess I have to live with.

I'm a mess.

"I can eat his face."

My heart lurches, hitting the roof of my mouth when Narsi hisses from next to me. I forgot how silently my sidekick can move when he is not resembling a tall hill of a monster. Stupidly, I thought I snuck away from him, too.

"You can't eat Eric's face, Narsi." Pressing the bridge of my nose does not help the headache throbbing at the back of my skull. "I kinda like it where it is."

"Shadow makes you uneasy. I do not like my Mistress in distress." My eyebrows climb up when he starts petting my leg lovingly. "I can eat half his face?" Those eyeless sockets lift to lock on my gaze. "Humans call it compromise."

"Now you decide to adopt some human mannerisms?" Keeping my tone low, I mutter under my breath while keeping an eye on the front entrance of the safe house through a crack in the door, which is clutched in my white-knuckled grip. "This is not up for debate. How about not eating anyone for a while. Let's start with that."

Eric, his brother, and Beelzebub march inside the house with purpose, and that's enough proof for me to justify my idea of hiding. They are up to something, and I'll bet my horns and tail it has something to do with me. My suspicions are confirmed when the twins shoulder their way behind Beelzebub and shove him forward to lead the way. Oh, yeah. Eric is definitely planning to corner me if his arrogant, grumpy ass is willing to walk behind the others. Any other time, nothing will prevent him from finding me.

"Hel," Beelzebub bellows from the top of his lungs, his boots thumping rhythmically over the hardwood floors. "I brought your mate back unharmed. He might've cried a couple of times, but nothing we can't fix. Where are you?"

Lips pressed in a firm line, I stay quiet and watch them search for me, the doors opening and closing with more force the longer they come out empty-handed. Meanwhile,

Narsi snickers gleefully next to me, his tiny body vibrating from excitement because they are getting angry. It'll be a clusterfuck in less then five minutes, but I stubbornly refuse to face them. I'm doing great ignoring everything, thank you very much, and I'd like to keep it that way.

I know the jig is up when they get Raphael to join them.

Steeling my spine, I take a deep breath and yank the door open. "Oh great, you're all back." Stepping out in the hallway, I start backing toward the entrance when all four of them poke their heads out from different rooms. "I'll go find George and Cass, and we can meet up in the common area in like an hour. Hold the forte while I'm gone." I add two thumbs up for good measure.

Spinning on my heel, I bolt for the door, but Narsi is still clinging to my damn leg, so I almost faceplant before I reach it. My shriek is cut short when a familiar calloused hands wrap around my upper arms and pulls me to a firm, unyielding chest. When Eric's scent fills my nose and my head spins from the instant need I have for him, I know my escape is not meant to be. While my brain screams for me to run and not allow them to drag me into a conversation better left alone, my body has a different plan. It turns pliant in my mate's arms, molding to him like it's meant to be in his embrace. Which I suppose is the truth of it.

"Eric, there you are." Turning inside the circle of his arms, I plant a kiss on his soft lips, and his hold loosens around me. "You rest, lover, and I'll be right back." Ducking out of his embrace while he struggles to hold back his reaction, I take one step before he yanks me back.

"And where do you think you are going, Hel?" His deep voice raises goosebumps over my arms. "The hunters are on their way. We saw them from the sky when we were returning here."

"Right." I stop struggling and offer him a strained smile. "I'll just meet them outside the wards then, just to make sure nothing is following behind them."

The house spins around, and I'm thrown over a shoulder before I'm done talking. Narsi the traitor snickers when I lift my head to glare at him through the curtain of my hair, doing some deranged happy dance with his arms flopping as he jumps in a circle. One second he wants to eat Eric's face, and the next he is okay with my mate manhandling me to wherever he feels I should be going. To add insult to injury, Eric's hand connects with my ass with a loud smack, the sting of the slap rendering me mute for a second. It speaks volumes of my mental state that I don't rip him a new one until he deposits me on my feet in the space we use for meetings.

The room is empty of everything but a long, wooden table they drug from what was left of Sanctuary and the mismatched chairs sprinkled around it. Maps marked with red and yellow lines connecting the closed and opened portals around Atlanta and her neighboring areas are spread all over it. Refusing to look at any of them, I fist my hands and stare at the spiderwebbed cracks in the empty walls above their heads. It's easy to do because all four are blocking the door in case I try to escape again.

"Okay, fine. Let's hear it." When the silence stretches to the point of driving me nuts, I fold my arms across my chest. My damn tail twitches around my waist, and my butt cheeks clench from its movement. "Out with it."

"Shadow is worried about you." Beelzebub grins like a fiend, his red eyes glittering with amusement when Eric snarls at him. "You decided I'll be the one to talk to her. I never said I won't throw you under the bus for it." One meaty shoulder rolls in the semblance of a shrug before he turns his focus back to me. "Now that I have made sure he is the one who will pay for this, I have to say we all are worried. Much as I hate to admit it, I worry about you too." Squeezing the words through clenched teeth, I watch in fascination as a muscle jumps in his square jaw.

Raphael mentioned a few times that Beelzebub is not too pleased with his concern of my wellbeing, but until now, I thought he was just trying to add to my guilt for refusing to talk with them. Locked in the Archdemon's red gaze, all my attempts to calm the galloping of my heart are futile, which doesn't go unnoticed by any of them. But what can I tell them that they don't already know? Apart from why Eric and Raphael are both standing in this room, they know most of what eats me alive.

"I have no idea what you guys want me to say." Throwing my arms up in defeat, I stomp to the table and plop my ass on the edge. Narsi inches closer and reaches for my leg, but my glare stops him from touching me. The little shit needs to learn not to switch sides when it suits him. "We failed. No matter how you look at it, because of me, the human realm paid the price. Just look around you. Was I worth all the lives lost?"

"Yes," all four answer in a choir and stare at me unblinking.

It becomes obvious I'm going to carry this weight alone because they don't understand the gravity of our actions. For them, including Raphael, a human life is but a blink of an eye and not something to mourn. If I'm being honest with myself, I haven't come to terms with my immortality yet, but I do remember all too well how aware I was of my mortal body and soul before my life turned upside down. Not long ago, I was one of the humans, regardless if that was true or not. I grew up believing I was one of those standing between them and all evil. Just because my concept of what is evil has changed doesn't mean my sense of responsibility has. Heaven, Hell, Purgatory … they can all gouge their eyes out for all I care as long as they leave the human realm alone.

They didn't.

"I'm sorry I can't agree with you on that." Rubbing my forehead, I blow out a deep breath through pursed lips. "I can't see what's left out there"—My hand shoots out, pointing in a random direction—"and think, you know what? I'm just happy that I'm alive. To hell with all the innocents who died in the process. At first it was Abaddon, then it was the jinn, but we all must face the truth now. It was us. We did this." Swallowing the lump that formed in my throat, I don't hide my anguish from them anymore. "I did this."

"Hel." Raphael doesn't need to say anything else for me to know he is as tortured by everything that happened as I am. It's clear as day in the tone of his voice.

"No." Eric, on the other hand, has a different opinion, as always. Of course he does when it comes to me. "I will not apologize for what any of us have done. This is all on the jinn and their twisted ideas of how the realms should be. Their hunger for power is what brought us to this. A lot of lives were lost, but look at how many we have saved." With each word, he moves closer until he looms over me, and I have to crane my neck to keep eye contact. "If you want someone else to blame, then blame it on me, Hel. Because I'll tell you this once again and for the last time. I'll do it all over again and kill them all to have you here with me. I will not apologize for that. Not ever."

"As much as I love disagreeing with Eric, I have to say he makes a valid point." Raphael braves coming shoulder to shoulder with my mate. "I did the unspeakable for you, and as much as it left a mark on my very existence, I do not regret it. I can't."

"We will have to agree to disagree then." Squirming under their scrutiny, I kick Narsi away when he latches onto my leg. "No hugging now that you are not bothered by them lecturing me."

"I like my Mistress alive." My sidekick pouts, but he doesn't look apologetic at all. "You said I cannot eat Shadow's face."

The incredulous expression on Eric's face is worth all the discomfort I suffered from the conversation.

"As much as I'd love to see the Haltija munch on my brother, I would have to agree with them, she-devil. You are a pain in my ass, but the realms need you." I watch Colt saunter to the closest chair and sprawl on it, spreading his legs wide and throwing an arm over the back of it. "The human realm will recover as it always does. The damn things procreate like rabbits if you ask me. If we did nothing, it could've been much worse."

"Instead of dwelling on what could've been, maybe we should look into where Lucifer is." Beelzebub takes a page from Colt's book and grabs a chair for himself too, straddling it. "With him still missing and Leviathan who knows where, I doubt Satanael can create any sort of order in Hell. We have Michael missing as well, don't we? That makes Hell and Heaven ready to go boom at any moment. If that happens, all we did will be for nothing."

I never thought of it that way, but now anxiety churns in my stomach. For whatever reason, I dumbly believed everything was over and we just had to help rebuild the human realm. How stupid of me to think the Fates will make it as easy as all that. They let me keep Eric and Raphael, but my fight is not over. The question is, how do I go about it? Like it or not, I have to admit them forcing me to face my short-comings might just save me from carrying even more guilt on my shoulders.

"Your mother lives."

With a thick swallow, I nod at Beelzebub. "You are right. We should look for them."

"Great." Colt jumps to his feet. "I know just where to start."

The Fates help us when we need Eric's twin to lead the way.

Grab your copy...
vinci-books.com/devilhisdue

About the Author

Maya Daniels, USA Today Bestselling and multi-award-winning supernatural suspense author, is a fun-loving woman with many talents.

She traveled the world, gaining life experiences that helped her career as an investigative journalist, as well as her storytelling. Maya writes compelling tales of magic, mythical creatures, loyalty, and life-changing friendships with snarky female characters—much like herself.

Her travels have taken her to Europe, Africa, Asia, Australia, and America. Born with her feet in motion, she currently resides in Ohio, spinning her next epic story that you will not want to put down.

Her biggest 'sins' are her love of chocolate and coffee—through an IV drip! One to never sit still, Maya practices Reiki healing, different types of martial arts, reads about the arcane, talks to furry creatures more than humans, picks up a sledgehammer for home improvement, and travels with her fated mate, seeking her own adventures.